ICE MAIDEN

On the same day that she's made redundant, Kat Ingram learns that River Farm, their family home for generations, may have to be sold. To top it all, George Logan, from neighbouring Stoneygates Farm, proposes marriage as a way to help save River Farm. Kat decides to visit her sister in Canada, where she meets and falls for wealthy artist Ambrose Legris. When George tries a more romantic approach, Kat must decide — talented, arrogant Ambrose, or safe, dependable George?

CATRIONA McCUAIG

ICE MAIDEN

Complete and Unabridged

LINFORD
Leicester

First published in Great Britain in 2003

First Linford Edition
published 2006

British Library CIP Data

McCuaig, Carol Bennett, *1938* –
    Ice maiden.—Large print ed.—
Linford romance library
1. Love stories
2. Large type books
I. Title
823.9'2 [F]

ISBN 1–84617–411–2

Published by
F. A. Thorpe (Publishing)
Anstey, Leicestershire

Set by Words & Graphics Ltd.
Anstey, Leicestershire
Printed and bound in Great Britain by
T. J. International Ltd., Padstow, Cornwall

This book is printed on acid-free paper

1

Kat Ingram returned to her work station with a sinking heart. Outside the office, the rain was thudding down out of a leaden sky — perfectly appropriate weather to accompany bad news, she thought.

She had just come from a meeting in which the managing director of their firm had delivered his message with a face to match the weather, all doom and gloom. He had emphasised the economy, competition from abroad and downsizing. Kat hardly listened. She knew the form — last in, first out. She was about to be made redundant! It didn't help that the man had put off the inevitable until Christmas was over. It was January now and the blow had fallen.

'You as well?'

Her neighbour, Toni, looked across

with a wry expression, waving the notification she had just torn from its envelope.

'Old Tompkins didn't have the nerve to tell us face to face which of us has to go, he had to hand out little love notes instead.'

Kat pulled a face in return.

'It's a bit of a shock, getting a month's pay in lieu of notice. I mean, I got up this morning, expecting another day on the treadmill, and now we could be heading for the dole queue!'

'Better than having to come in here for the next few weeks, I'd say, with all the lucky ones giving us pitying looks! In fact, I don't think I'll bother waiting for five o'clock. Somebody else can do these rotten invoices. If I rush, I can catch the ten-fifty home.'

Toni began to burrow in her desk drawer, sorting out her personal belongings.

'Should I leave this cheese sandwich behind for old Tompkins?' she quipped. 'If things are as bad as he makes out, he might be glad of it!'

She flounced out, leaving Kat staring fixedly at her blank computer screen, as if a solution to her problems might appear there by magic.

Later, waiting at the bus stop for what seemed an age, she gave way to her misery. She had forgotten her umbrella that morning and, despite her thick cloche hat, her chestnut hair was hanging in rats' tails and some icy drops had worked their way under her coat collar and were running down her back.

She longed to get home where she could thaw out in their big farm kitchen while her mother dispensed tea and sympathy, and perhaps some freshly-baked scones with home-made jam. This comfortable vision faded when she turned in at the gate, where a car stood, polished and gleaming in the downpour. Nigel! What was he doing here on a weekday afternoon?

Her mother looked up in surprise when Kat opened the kitchen door.

'You're early, dear. Anything wrong?'

'Tell you later, Mum. Have to get out of these wet things!'

She nodded at her brother, who responded with a grunt.

Ten minutes later, dressed in a thick red polo-necked jumper, shabby corduroy trousers and ancient sheepskin slippers, she returned to the kitchen in time to hear Nigel pontificating about income and outgoings while their mother listened with a glazed expression. Apparently Mr Tompkins wasn't the only one with concerns about the economy. Nigel, the accountant, seemed to be on the same wavelength.

'Any tea in the pot, Mum?'

Rose Ingram took the lid off the big brown teapot and peered inside.

'Better make a fresh pot, dear, and make it strong! We could all do with it after what Nigel's been telling me.'

'Not for me, Mother, I must be on my way,' Nigel said. 'Now, do give some thought to what I've been saying, and I'll call in next week on my way to

Worcester, and you can tell me what decision you've arrived at.'

When the sound of the car's engine had died away, Kat looked at her mother, who was staring out of the window, white-faced. She had come home to weep on her mother's shoulder, but evidently that would now have to wait. Her mother pushed her cup across the table for a refill.

'So, what did Nigel have to say?' Kat asked.

'Oh, you know Nigel, full of jargon I couldn't understand. What it all boils down to is that River Farm is in trouble. We're spending more money than we take in.'

'But how can that be? I thought things have been jogging along much as usual.'

Her mother sighed.

'Things haven't been the same since your father died. Oh, we've done our best, and it was so good of you to give up your job to come home to help, finding a post which pays far less. Never think I don't appreciate it. It's just that we really need another man now. It's hard to manage with just the two of us and poor old Simon, and that's why I asked Nigel to look over the books, to see if we couldn't take on someone else. However, it appears that we can barely afford to pay Simon, much less hire a younger man who'd ask a better wage. That's if we could find one! Agricultural labourers are hardly thick on the ground!'

'Isn't Simon about due for retirement?' Kat mused. 'He's been here for ever. I certainly can't remember a time when he wasn't here.'

'As far as I know, Simon is seventy-two,' her mother told her. 'He could have given up a long time ago, but I think he wants to soldier on as long as possible. I did say something at one point and he looked me straight in the eye and asked me in that blunt way of his if we wanted to get rid of him. Of course, I had to say no, and even if he has slowed down a bit one has to admit that he's a dab hand with machinery. And that's another thing,' she went on, scrabbling in the biscuit tin. 'That tractor is on its last legs, and new ones don't grow on trees.'

'So what was it that Nigel wanted you to think about?'

'Selling up! Can you imagine? He wants me to sell River Farm!'

The rain eased off and Kat, dressed in her mac and wellingtons, set out for a walk, with old Gyp at her heels. With so much on her mind she felt as if her head would burst. Walking through the woods, staring up at the bare trees, she longed for spring to come. Things always looked better in that season of hope, with new life springing up on every side.

As she neared the line of fences which separated their land from Stoneygates Farm next door, Gyp surged forward with a bark and she was glad to see George Logan striding towards her, followed by his dog, Shep. Shep and Gyp were brother and sister, part of a long line of sheepdogs born at Stoneygates.

Kat and George had known each other all their lives. When George was a child his parents had assumed he'd be a perfect companion for Nigel, but the two boys had never got on. Nigel was keen on model trains and adventure stories, George was interested in wild-life and boating on the river. His sister, Dorothy, went everywhere in company with Kat's elder sister, Christina, and, in a country place where there were no other children close by, George and Kat became fast friends. Luckily they both had sensible parents and nobody was interested in telling Kat to spend time with her dolls, or to bully George into playing football.

'Nice evening!' George said now, as they came to a halt on opposite sides of the stile.

Kat nodded, and George picked up on her mood immediately.

'Bad day at work?' he enquired, his head on one side.

'You could say that. I've been made redundant. Life as we know it came to an end when I walked out of that office at twelve o'clock today.'

'Oh, lor!' he said sympathetically. 'Does Rose know?'

'Not yet. I haven't found the right moment. I came rushing home with the news, only to find that Nigel had got in first.'

'Don't tell me Mr Wonderful has got the sack!'

'No, no, nothing like that. We have, though. Nigel says we ought to sell River Farm.'

George said nothing. He knew only too well how difficult it was to make a living from farming these days. They were doing all right at Stoneygates, but then his father was still hale and hearty, and had his two sons to work with him. They had no need of hired help, and George supposed that was the trouble with the Ingrams. It had been a great disappointment to Joe Ingram when Nigel had declared he wasn't cut out for farming and had swanned off to train as an accountant. Still, if his heart wasn't in the land he wouldn't have made a good farmer anyway.

'We can't possibly sell up,' Kat went on. 'This place has been in the family for two hundred years. I can't bear to think of other people living here, making changes. We'll just have to think of something.'

'You could marry me, and we could run the two places together,' George said, in all seriousness, but Kat laughed.

'That would be the perfect solution. Three men for the price of one! Imagine me walking into the kitchen and being able to tell Mum that all our troubles are over.'

She looked back over the fields, seeing her old home in the distance.

'I love that house so much,' she said softly. 'When I was little I used to imagine all the people who must have lived there over the years, generations of Ingrams and all their little girls like myself. In the back of my mind I always knew I'd have to leave it some day, just as Tina did when she got married, yet I believed it would always be there, waiting for me.'

'You don't have to leave it, Kat. We could live there with your mother. I'm sure she wouldn't mind.'

Kat swung round to face him, her eyes wide.

'Oh, George, I thought you were just talking, the way we always do. You weren't serious, were you?'

She broke off when she saw the expression on his face.

'I meant every word of it, Kat. I suppose I could have picked a better time and place to ask you, moonlight and roses and all that, but when you told me your news . . . '

His voice trailed off.

Kat looked at her old friend, searching for the right words, wanting to turn him down without inflicting unnecessary hurt. George was so trustworthy and safe, standing there in his old tweed jacket and khaki trousers, his straight brown hair blowing in the wind. He was as familiar and dear to her as the land on which they stood. How easy it would be to marry him and fall in with his plans, but that was not enough.

'I'm so sorry, George. It's wonderful of you to ask me, but I can't say yes. I'm very fond of you, but I'm not in love with you, you see. It wouldn't be fair to marry you.'

'Not even to save the farm?' George quipped.

Kat smiled at him, her eyes full of pain.

'You deserve better, someone who'd really love you, George. Don't settle for half measures.'

'Oh, well, it was worth a try, and you know me, I don't give up that easily.'

He changed the subject then, asking her if she wanted to go to the Young Farmers' dance with him, and the awkward moment passed.

Kat hastened home in the gathering

dusk, her mind whirling with conflicting emotions. It had been quite a day. Why couldn't she have taken the easy way out? George's suggestion seemed to provide answers yet she knew that her reaction had been the right one. He did deserve something better than a woman who looked on him as a brother.

As for Kat, she had never been in love, but she knew she'd recognise it when it came. Love was feeling weak at the knees and seeing shooting stars. George had kissed her on several occasions in the past, all very pleasurable, but there had certainly been no fireworks.

2

The curtains were drawn and Kat and her mother were seated in front of a blazing fire with Gyp snoring at their feet. Rose was knitting a bright red jersey for her grandson in Canada. Christina and her husband, Tom Frye, lived near Ottawa and had two small children, Lucy and Jack.

'So what does Nigel have in mind, exactly?' Kat asked, staring into the leaping flames, comforted by the glow.

'He thinks we should either sell this as a working farm or, if that fails, sell off the house with a couple of acres and see if the neighbours are interested in adding a field or two to their own properties.'

'And what about us? Where are we supposed to go? Off to the knacker's yard like a couple of broken-down, old horses?'

'Not quite,' Rose replied, pushing her spectacles back up her nose. 'He said I could go into sheltered housing, leaving you free to go back to London. I'm not ready for retirement yet, thank you very much, I told him, so then he said what about emigrating to Canada? Tom and Tina have a spare bedroom. Well, so do he and Rosemary, but I notice they haven't offered to take in the aged granny!'

'Aged granny, my foot!' Kat snapped.

Rose was barely sixty and, having worked on the farm all her married life, was as fit as any younger woman who worked out in a gym.

'I must say, though, I've always felt badly that you had to give up your fine job in London to come home after your father died. Hewitt & Preen don't pay nearly as much, I know.'

While that was true, Kat hadn't minded. During her first days in London she'd been thrilled by all the sights and sounds — Buckingham Palace, Trafalgar Square, the famous art

15

galleries and theatres. The one draw-back was that accommodation was so expensive. She'd longed for a tastefully-furnished flat but had had to settle for a lonely bedsitter miles from her place of work, which meant a daily rush for the Underground.

'Yes, well, there's something I have to tell you about Hewitt & Preen,' she began.

Her mother's face fell at the news.

'It never rains but it pours.' She sighed. 'What will you do now, then, go back to London?'

'I've been thinking about that, but perhaps this was meant to be, losing my job, I mean. It means I can stay here and help you on the farm.'

'Oh, Kat!'

Rose dropped a stitch and had to fiddle with her knitting before going on with her thoughts.

'Much as I'd love to have you here full time it still wouldn't solve all our financial problems. If only I were a bit younger I could get some sort of job, then the fields could be sold and at least we might save the house. It's no good wishing, of course. People just don't give jobs to people of my age.'

'It's too bad I turned George down,' Kat mused, regretting having said this as soon as the words were out of her mouth as her mother brightened at once.

'George has proposed? How absolutely lovely! Do you know, your poor father always hoped that the pair of you might make a go of it some day.'

Stopping Rose Ingram in mid-flow was like trying to dam a river in full spate, but Kat managed it.

'Steady on, Mum. I told you, I turned him down.'

'Oh, well, it never does to appear too eager. He'll ask you again, I'm sure.'

Kat thought it best to change the subject.

'There must be lots of things we could do on top of real farming. Things you and I could do as a team, like farm holidays, bed and breakfast, making jams and baked goods for sale.'

Rose nodded. This wasn't the time to throw cold water on Kat's plans. After all, the poor girl had just lost her job. However, all that sounded like a great deal of work for two pairs of hands, and where was the start-up capital to come from? Bed-and-breakfast guests expected a certain standard of comfort and the house, not to mention its contents, was woefully shabby. And surely American guests would want en suite bathrooms.

Fortunately, this train of thought was interrupted by the ringing of the telephone. Reluctantly Rose left the warmth of the fireside and went out to the freezing hall. Minutes later she put her head round the door.

'It's Christina, wanting to speak to you.'

'Why me?'

'Come along and find out and look sharp. She's phoning all the way from Canada,' she added unnecessarily.

'Why are you calling me at this time

of night?' Kat wanted to know.

'And hello to you, too! And it's afternoon here, if you must know. As a matter of fact, Nigel called me this morning. He wants me to talk Mum into selling the farm. He has it all planned, as usual. Mum is to move in with us, and the process of the sale will be divided between us all. You'd get a share, too, of course.'

'Nice of him!'

'Yes, well, you know Nigel. The thing is, we'd love to have Mum here, but that isn't the point. We mustn't let her be railroaded into anything.'

'She can't be made to sell, can she?' Kat asked anxiously.

'I doubt it, unless she does something silly, like signing papers supplied by Nigel, without reading them properly.'

'Surely he wouldn't go that far.'

'We'll have to see that he doesn't. Anyway, sorry to hear about your job and all that.'

'Bad news travels fast!'

'Mum just mentioned it in passing.

And I gather that congratulations are in order?'

'I see she told you that, too! And did she also tell you that I turned him down?'

'Poor George.'

Christina waited patiently while her younger sister explained how she felt. Then she went on.

'I've got a great idea. Let me give you something else to think about, Kat, and then I must run. This call is costing me money.'

Rose was knitting placidly when Kat returned, shivering, to her armchair.

'Tina wants me to fly over for a few weeks,' Kat told her.

'In January? Be a bit beastly there at this time of year, won't it?'

'February, actually, by the time I go. According to her, Ottawa has a winter festival with all kinds of interesting outdoor events, including ice skating, fabulous ice sculptures, you name it. Winterlude, they call it, or the Bal de Neige. People come from all over the world to see it. The hotels are all booked up months in advance.'

'Why not go then? You can put your severance pay towards the cost of the aeroplane ticket.'

'We need that money here, Mum.'

'Now, none of that!' Rose spoke firmly. 'It will give you a bit of breathing space. Time enough to think about the future of this place when you get back. And,' she added, 'if you do take on another job you won't be due any holidays for ages, so you may as well have one now, while you've got the chance.'

Kat sat back, her eyes sparkling. Mum was right. Why not go to Canada? She had never been abroad, apart from a school trip to France, and this would be an adventure.

'And if you go,' Rose continued, with an air of one making a great pronounce-ment, 'you can take this pullover with you, and save me the cost of postage!'

'Done!' Kat cried, startling Gyp out of a sound sleep. 'I'll visit the travel agency tomorrow.'

3

The Fryes' home was on the edge of a pleasant Ottawa suburb, overlooking woods and fields.

'It's ideal for us,' Christina enthused, as she showed Kat over the house. 'Just a short run into the city for Tom to get to work and a good bus service for when I want to go shopping downtown. It's not real country, of course, but it's the next best thing.'

'It looks like real country to me,' Kat said, looking out on a picture postcard scene of evergreen trees, their branches weighed down with heavy snow.

'There are groomed trails all through that woodland. People use them for cross-country skiing and for jogging and dog walking the rest of the year.'

Christina turned away from the window and began opening drawers.

'I've emptied these for you, and if you need more space you can let me know, although you don't seem to have brought much with you. You can borrow things from me. It's a good job we're the same size. When the temperature drops to thirty below zero one needs more than wellies and an anorak.'

Kat was keen to sample all the winter fun that Canada had to offer. Her brother-in-law, who was an avid down-hill skier, offered to take her to one of the nearby ski resorts, where she could take lessons on the nursery slopes, but she wasn't sure about this.

'I don't want a broken leg to add to my other troubles,' she teased.

Tom grinned.

'Better stick to cross country, then. You'll probably have a few falls at first, but that won't do you any harm.'

So Kat found herself shuffling along on borrowed skis, feeling awkward while her nephew, Jack, skimmed by her on a miniature pair.

'Look at me, Auntie!' the four-year-old shouted, as he propelled himself forward.

'We'll have this one on skis next winter,' Christina observed, nodding towards two-year-old Lucy, who was riding comfortably in a sling on her father's back.

'Don't remind me,' Kat groaned. 'If this is so easy, why can't I get the hang of it?'

'Patience, woman,' Tom told her. 'It's all a question of getting into a rhythm. You come out here every day and you'll be an expert in no time.'

Kat looked forward to going into Ottawa to see the various events in the winter festival that she'd heard so much about.

'It's held on three consecutive weekends,' her sister explained. 'The weather can be unpredictable at this time of year and a thaw can happen at any time, ruining the sculptures and wiping out all the activities which need freezing conditions. That could be disastrous for the organisers. People come from all over the world for this and a lot of time and money goes into it. By spreading the festival over a three-week period they have a better chance of success.'

With Tom at work all day, Christina lived a busy life of her own, mostly bound up with the children. She took them to playgroup several mornings a week and Kat was left to her own devices. She planned to use the time to practise her skiing.

It was a crisp morning when she went out early on the trails for the third time. The sun was shining out of an incredibly blue sky as she glided along, meeting nobody. Well-used trails branched off from the main path. Christina had explained that the area was honeycombed with such detours, but Kat had no way of knowing where they led. Perhaps she should explore a bit, she thought. She couldn't actually get lost while her tracks were still visible.

One trail looked particularly inviting.

It led through an open gate and from there wound up a gentle slope towards a grove of cedars. Just the place to practise the climbing technique Tom had taught her.

Everything then happened at once. An enormous dog appeared out of nowhere, barking furiously. Alarmed, Kat lost her balance and landed in a huddle in the snow, just as a tall figure appeared over the hill.

'Bruce! Heel! Here, boy!'

The dog backed off, growling, as a man skimmed downhill, coming to a graceful halt inches away from where Kat lay in a crumpled heap.

'What the devil do you think you're doing?' he demanded furiously.

Resisting the urge to utter a sarcastic reply, Kat swallowed her annoyance and spoke calmly.

'I was going along, minding my own business, when your dog suddenly leaped at me.'

Struggling unsuccessfully to get up she felt at a distinct disadvantage. The beastly man could at least help her up, she thought, but he made no move towards her and she lay where she had fallen, glaring up at him. There was no way she was going to beg! But he wasn't finished.

'Bruce had every right to warn you off. He's been trained to run trespassers off my land.'

'I didn't know I was trespassing. Isn't this a branch off the main trail?'

He looked down grimly. In a different setting he might have appeared wickedly good looking, with his black hair and dark eyes, but at that moment his mouth was curled in a sneer which made him look very much like his ferocious dog.

'A closed gate usually denotes private property, mam'selle, but you are as bad as all the rest. You people think you have the right to enter where you don't belong, leaving gates open for my sheep to stray.'

This was too much.

'I live on a farm myself and I know

better than to leave gates open, even when there are no animals in sight. And if you take a look at your gate you'll see that it must have been standing open for some time, judging by the condition of the snow.'

He gazed at her for a long moment before executing a neat turn on his skis and moving off in the direction he had come, with the dog loping ahead of him. He looked back once.

'You can close the gate on your way out,' he called, leaving Kat fuming.

Blinking back tears of frustration she tried to get up, only managing to snap one of her bamboo poles in the attempt. Finally, after unfastening the skis she managed to scramble upright, landing on her hands and knees in deep snow. At last she was on her way, the seat of her trousers uncomfortably clammy as a result of her tumble. That arrogant man! For two pins she'd leave the gate the way she'd found it, but her country upbringing was too deeply ingrained in her for that. She struggled

28

with the heavy wooden thing and then set out for home.

She returned to a minor crisis, however! The house seemed to be full of wailing children.

'It's my friend, Shelley,' Christina bawled, over the roar of outraged infants. 'Her mother's had a stroke and been rushed to hospital and Shelley's gone there to be with her, so I'm taking care of the brood until her husband gets home. Samantha, no!'

She swooped down on a toddler who was busily engaged in trying to put baked beans up her brother's nose. The noise went up several decibels.

'Just let me get into dry clothes and I'll give you a hand,' Kat told her.

'What?'

'Never mind. Be back in a minute.'

The rest of the afternoon was spent trying to keep Samantha, Tiffany and Pinky amused. Jack, usually an amiable little fellow, had turned into a small devil, showing off in front of the visitors. All in all, there was no opportunity for Kat to tell her sister about her encounter with the unpleasant farmer in the woods. She made up her mind that if their paths ever crossed again she would tell him exactly what she thought of his uncouth behaviour. However, as she was returning home at the end of the month it was unlikely that they'd meet again.

'Try not to be late home this evening, Tom,' his wife warned him, as he left the breakfast table to go warm up the car.

'I'll do my best, unless I get held up in traffic,' he told her, reaching for his goose-down parka.

Christina turned to Kat.

'A few of our friends are coming in for drinks this evening. We don't usually entertain much during the winter. One never knows what the roads will be like. We're making an exception because you've come. Everyone wants to meet you, and they're all feeling a bit flat now that Christmas and New Year are behind us, so this

30

will cheer everyone up.'

'Lovely, I'll wear my new dress,' Kat replied.

She had splurged on a full-skirted dark green dress to wear to the firm's Christmas party and had received many compliments from her colleagues and their spouses. Not only did it look well on her slim figure, setting off her shining chestnut hair, it was also quite versatile, depending on what she did to dress it up. She had come prepared with some gold chains and some pretty silk scarves so she had plenty of choice.

'I'll have to pop into town this morning,' Christina went on. 'We need some bits and pieces. I don't suppose . . . '

Kat knew what was coming next.

'Yes, I'll keep an eye on the children here. You'll have an easier time if you go on your own. I'd volunteer to go for you, but of course I don't know my way around the shops.'

'You're an angel,' Christina told her. 'Jack is at the stage where he takes goodies off the shelves and makes a fuss when he's made to put them back. If you can keep them from wrecking the house while I'm gone I'll be delighted.'

She had no sooner left the house when the phone rang. It was Shelley.

'Thank goodness you're at home. Is Tina there?'

'I'm afraid not. She had to pop into town, but she shouldn't be too long, if you'd like to call back later.'

'What I'm really phoning for is to ask if she can have the kids again this afternoon. Mum's taken a turn for the worse and I really need to be at the hospital.'

'Oh, dear.'

Kat didn't quite know what to say. With guests coming it simply wasn't convenient to let three more youngsters under the age of four loose in Christina's immaculate home. She hurriedly made arrangements to help Shelley.

'You've done what?'

Christina, cold and exhausted, reached

for the coffee pot while fending off her daughter's sticky fingers.

'Trot along and wash those hands, please, Lucy. You're getting jam all over my nice coat.'

'I felt sorry for the woman,' Kat explained. 'She's so worried about her poor mother, and I knew you couldn't have them here because of the party. And that's another thing, I took care not to mention that as she isn't invited.'

'Well, of course I didn't invite her when poor Mrs Crisp is so ill. So now you're stuck with going over to Shelley's to babysit the three terrors, when you're supposed to be the guest of honour at this party!'

'It's only until Shelley's husband gets home. I'll be back in plenty of time for a nice, long soak in the bath, and shampoo my hair.'

But John Fellowes failed to arrive at the expected time and Kat had his children fed and bedded before his car finally turned into the driveway. Full of apologies, he headed straight for the drinks cabinet, offering perfunctory thanks and asking how much he owed her.

'I'm not a paid sitter,' she said stiffly, and fled.

Stumbling down the street, having difficulty keeping her footing on the slippery sidewalk, she felt like the White Rabbit, telling herself that she was horribly late. Cars were lined up along the street and lights streamed from every window of the Fryes' house. The guests had obviously beaten her to it. There wasn't time to take that leisurely bath and wash her hair. All she could hope for was to sneak up to her room unnoticed and change into her glad rags. She let herself in by the back door, shrugging off her coat as she went. She tiptoed into the hall, about to make a dash for the stairs.

Unfortunately the living-room door opened at that moment and Kat was faced with a room full of people, all staring at her with interest. Recovering her aplomb, Christina clapped her hands.

'She's here, everyone,' she exclaimed.

The nearest guest, a young woman in flowing robes, stepped forward, hand extended, and was introduced as Genevieve Legris.

'And this is my brother, Ambrose,' she said, standing aside to let him out into the hall.

'I believe we've already met,' he said drily.

Standing there, perfectly groomed right down to his shiny black shoes, was the farmer from the woods! He looked Kat up and down quizzically, taking in her dishevelled appearance. Her jumper was stained with milk where Pinky had burped up his supper, and her slacks were covered in grey hairs, picked up from the Fellowes' cat. Kat's heart sank. Once again this man had managed to place her at a disadvantage.

'Do excuse me, I must go and change,' she blurted out, and bolted upstairs.

4

'Mummy! I want a drink of water!' Jack's plaintive voice came floating down the stairs making Christina pause in her work of stacking plates in the dishwasher.

'Go up to him, Tom, will you? He'll have Lucy awake in a minute, and then we'll never get the pair of them off. He doesn't really need a drink, of course. He just wants to know what's going on.'

Tom found Jack's Winnie the Pooh mug and went upstairs. Christina peered into the living-room.

'Now, what's left to do? Still a few glasses in here. You can hand wash those if you will, Kat. I don't trust my good crystal to the machine.'

Kat was silent. Still in her smart green dress, with one of her sister's aprons protecting her from the soap suds, she looked elegant and sophisticated. If only Ambrose Legris had seen her like this! But by the time she had cleaned herself up and come downstairs he and his sister had left. Every time he thought of her, if indeed he did at all, he would have a mental vision of a grubby, wind-tossed young woman, a proper scruff!

'You're very quiet, Kat. Anything wrong?'

Kat jumped. Christina had a look of concern on her lovely face, and Kat knew from long experience what that meant.

'Come on, little sister, tell me what's the matter. You know I'll worm it out of you somehow!'

'It's nothing, really. Just that Ambrose Legris . . . '

'Ambrose! Why, you hardly spoke to each other. He and Genevieve had to go on. They were due at the opera, as it happened, so I don't understand what's wrong.'

'We've met before,' Kat muttered.

Christina stared at her, puzzled. There seemed to be more here than met the eye.

'Sit down right there,' she ordered. 'I'll put the kettle on, and make you a sandwich. You missed your evening meal, and with so many of our friends wanting to speak to you I doubt if you were able to fill up on finger food. Then I want to know exactly what you're talking about.'

With a strong cup of tea and a thick ham sandwich in front of her, Kat told her story.

'So you see, it was a shock to find him here, dressed up to the nines, and me looking like I'd been dragged through a hedge backwards. This is the second time the beastly man has managed to put me at a disadvantage.'

Christina laughed.

'You mustn't mind Ambrose. He can be a bit sharp at times, but he's all right underneath.'

'A bit sharp! The man was positively uncouth!'

'Oh, well, they have had quite a bit of trouble with trespassers, that I do know. And, as you are well aware, leaving farm gates open is a cardinal sin.'

Kat was not about to give in.

'He must have realised by now that I'm your sister, not a common sightseer. He could at least have apologised for the way he treated me the other day, setting his dog on me and then leaving me flat on my back in a snow bank!'

Christina laughed again.

'You hardly gave him the chance, haring off upstairs like that. Another cup of tea?'

Tom came back into the kitchen.

'I think he's off, finally. Little rascal, he fell asleep right in the middle of begging me to read. Luckily Lucy slept through all the uproar. Any tea left in that pot?'

'Help yourself,' his wife told him. 'Our Kat's just been telling me how she fell foul of dear Ambrose the other day. She strayed on to his land when she was out skiing and he let her have it with both barrels.'

'Oh, you don't want to let him worry you,' Tom said, helping himself to sugar. 'Thinks a lot of himself, does Ambrose, but just stand up to him and he'll back down fast enough.'

'I can't quite figure him out,' Kat mused. 'Somehow the idea of a farmer taking in the opera doesn't quite ring true. Not that farmers can't be cultured, of course,' she added hastily, 'but can you imagine Mr Logan sitting through all four acts of La Traviata when the cows want milking?'

'Oh, Ambrose isn't a farmer,' Tom said. 'Wherever did you get that idea?'

'Not a farmer! Then what was all that about livestock and gates left open?'

'Ambrose is an artist. His work is very well thought of, I understand, although I can't see it myself. Give me a good photograph any day.'

'And Genevieve is a craftsperson in her own right,' Christina chimed in. 'She does the most beautiful wall hangings, sort of modern-day tapestries. They command high prices because she does the whole process herself from start to finish. That's why they keep sheep. She spins and dries the wool herself and then she weaves the hangings on her loom.'

Kat digested this.

'It all sounds quite romantic. I can imagine the two of them sitting in a little log cabin working away side by side, at their loom and easel.'

'Wrong again,' Tom guffawed. 'The reality is a huge, old, stone house, practically a mansion, set in five hundred rolling acres, complete with barns and stables.'

Kat stared at her brother-in-law in disbelief.

'But how on earth? I'm quite sure that a few paintings and wall hangings, no matter how good, could never support a lifestyle like that.'

'Old money,' Christina told her. 'Ambrose and Christina are the last remaining members of a very wealthy

Montreal family. The house was originally built as a country retreat for their great-grandfather and when their parents died, Ambrose chose to sell their house in Montreal and live here instead.'

'So is that all that Ambrose does? His painting, I mean? He doesn't need to earn a living otherwise?'

'Got it in one,' Tom said cheerfully. 'Not like some of us, who have to drive into the city in all winds and weathers, to earn a crust.'

'And a very nice crust it is, too,' Kat told him, looking round Christina's bright and cosy kitchen.

'We think so, don't we, love?' Christina said. 'But we'd be the first to admit that we're not in the same league as Ambrose. Never mind, to each his own.'

Kat was forced to revise her ideas. Knowing that the loss of even one sheep or cow could pose a serious problem for a farmer, she had assumed that there was at least some excuse for

Ambrose's behaviour, enraged as he had been by the open gate. The fact that he was a wealthy man put a different complexion on it. Despite their artistic lifestyle, Ambrose and his sister probably had a house full of valuable heirlooms, inherited from their parents. Naturally they wouldn't want strangers snooping around the property. She said as much to Christina.

'Well, there have been a few burglaries in the district recently,' her sister admitted. 'And yes, Ambrose does have one or two paintings that are supposed to be worth thousands.'

'Not his own works, though,' Tom put in. 'Landscapes by famous Canadian artists. It's the old story. The painters didn't get much for their work at the time, but prices sky-rocketed after they were dead. Perhaps the same thing will happen to Ambrose's paintings fifty years from now!'

'Does he do landscapes, too, then?'

'I'm not sure what you'd call them,' Christina said. 'The ones I've seen are scenes with people in them, farmers waiting to buy and sell livestock at the sale barn, that sort of thing. The one I'd particularly like to have is a rather lovely thing with two children playing in an orchard, but it's out of our price range, I'm afraid. Ambrose explained to me once that by the time the paintings are professionally framed, and then the gallery owner takes his rather stiff commission, the retail price is far higher than the amount the artist actually receives. So of course the end product has to be pricey. Even with all his money he doesn't want to work for nothing, and I can't blame him.'

Kat thought about this for a moment.

'Couldn't you buy an unframed canvas directly from Ambrose?'

Christina opened her eyes wide.

'What, and give him the impression we're looking for bargains, just because he's a neighbour? Anyway, if I were an artist I'd be inclined to charge the regular price and keep the unearned commission for myself. And why not?'

'You always were backward in coming forward, my girl. Just ask him and see. He might surprise you.'

'So why don't you ask him, then? You seem to be on such good terms with him!'

Kat slapped her sister with the damp tea towel she was holding. Laughing, Christina suggested that it was time they all turned in.

'Morning comes early in this house, with those two rascals upstairs!'

However, Kat, snuggled down under the duvet, was unable to fall asleep. She was overtired from her hours of hard work, looking after the Fellowes' children. Anxious because their mother had suddenly disappeared, they had played up so much that she was exhausted before she had been there for an hour.

'I'm not sure now if I want children of my own,' she had groaned to Christina, only half in jest. 'I tried to keep them entertained, but they refused to settle down. They seemed to spend the whole time shrieking, and jumping up and down on the furniture.'

'It's different when they're your own,' her sister replied. 'My two drive me round the bend at times, but they're my own flesh and blood and I wouldn't be without them. Added to which, you have your own kids from day one, so you bond together. Anybody would be put off by Shelley's kids. She doesn't have a clue as to how to manage them, and the poor thing is pregnant again, I hear.'

Yes, Kat thought, as she thumped her pillow into an acceptable shape, she supposed that she would like children some day, perhaps a little girl who looked like herself, and a little boy who resembled his father. She could see them now, dressed in overalls and small rubber boots, and pullovers knitted by Rose, helping to bottle-feed orphan lambs or playing with kittens in the hay loft.

That, of course, depended on whether River Farm could be saved.

She couldn't imagine bringing up children in a city flat. But who would their father be? At this stage in her life, Kat had no idea, but as she drifted off to sleep two men seemed to float before her eyes. First there was the dependable, open-faced George, solid as an English oak tree, a man she knew through and through.

Then there was Ambrose Legris, wealthy, talented and arrogant. In her mind she dubbed him dark and dangerous, totally unsuitable, of course, yet she felt drawn to him in some primeval attraction. Was she already a little in love with him? Of course, she had to return to England before too long, but in the meantime, was there any harm in getting to know him a little better?

According to Christina, Genevieve had hinted that she might invite them all to dinner one evening. If that happened, Ambrose would see a totally different side to the little sister from England!

Kat rolled over and went to sleep, to dream uneasily of River Farm, where her mother was welcoming Genevieve as a bed-and-breakfast guest! The young Frenchwoman was explaining that she simply must have a room with en suite facilities, because she had come from a Canadian mansion and what was on offer here in England was simply not what she was used to!

5

At the weekend, the family headed to Ottawa, eager to take in some of the Winterlude activities. There was so much to see and do that they had to decide ahead of time which events they would participate in, and which to leave until the following weekend.

'We can't try to do everything at once because of the children,' Christina explained. 'It's no pleasure to be wandering around with tired and cranky children in tow, and I don't want to leave them with a sitter. Winterlude is for the whole family, anyway.'

'I suggest we take a quick run to Confederation Park to see the ice carvings,' Tom said, 'and then we can go skating on the canal. We want you to see as much as possible while you're here, Kat, and if the weather should turn mild next weekend the ice won't be at its best. That has been known to happen, February or not!'

So the children were bundled into their snowsuits and installed in the car. Tom packed a dear little scarlet box sleigh into the boot for the use of his daughter when they reached the canal.

Confederation Park was full of people of all ages, marvelling at the magnificent sculptures, carved out of ice.

'I didn't realise they'd be so huge!' Kat gasped.

A man standing nearby heard this and grinned at her in amazement.

'Each one is carved out of a three hundred pound block of ice,' he told her. 'Sculptors come from all over the world to take part in this, Sweden, Australia, France, you name it.'

But the children soon grew restless, being much too young to appreciate the skill that had gone into the making of the ice sculptures.

'Let's go skating now!' Jack insisted, tugging at his father's arm.

'All right, let's go!' Tom smiled.

'Wet's go!' Lucy echoed, and reluctantly Kat tore herself away from the enthralling carvings.

Perhaps she could catch a bus later in the week and return here for a longer stay. Apparently there were even more ice sculptures, done by Canadian carvers, in front of the Parliament buildings, and she wanted to see those, too. She was looking forward to skating on the canal. She had never tried ice skating before, but she had been pretty good on roller skates when she was younger. Surely there wasn't much difference.

Even though Tom had told her what to expect she couldn't believe her eyes when they reached the canal, where hundreds of people were skating.

'Won't the ice crack under all those people?' she asked fearfully.

Christina laughed.

'No chance of that! It's tested regularly and whenever there's a thaw and it's believed to be unsafe, they warn people off until the temperature drops again. I know what you mean, though. When I first came to Canada and saw lorries being driven across the lakes I was absolutely horrified, but everyone assured me that with the ice being several feet thick it was quite safe.'

The scene was a mass of colour as people sped by, dressed in bright clothing. Couples were skating along arm in arm, parents pushed toddlers in sleighs, and there was even one brave old man shuffling along behind what looked like a kitchen chair. There was an enticing smell of food wafting from the kiosks manned by various vendors.

During the drive to Ottawa, Tom had explained that the Rideau Canal, built in the early nineteenth century to link Ottawa with Lake Ontario at Kingston, was over two hundred kilometres long.

'It's a busy waterway in summer, of course. When the children are a bit older and can be trusted not to fall overboard, we hope to hire a houseboat and take a holiday down through the

Rideau Lakes. I'm sure young Jack here would be thrilled to see all the boats going through the locks.'

'You go on ahead and keep an eye on Jack,' Christina told her husband, as he laced up Jack's skates. 'I'll stay with Kat until she finds her sea legs. We'll all meet back here later for eats and hot chocolate.'

'Hurray!' Jack shouted, as he staggered on to the ice, with his father close behind him.

Having laced up her hired skates, Kat was ready for action. The sisters made their way on to the ice, with little Lucy warmly wrapped up inside her sleigh, underneath a blanket. They hadn't gone very far before Lucy became agitated.

'Potty, Mummy!' she insisted, trying to struggle to her feet.

'Oh, no!' Christina sighed. 'It never fails. You ask them if they have to go to the toilet and they always say no. Then as soon as you get them all wrapped up in snowsuits and boots and all the rest of their winter gear, they have to go.

Roll on summer, I say. I'm so sorry, Kat, I'll have to take her back.'

'Don't worry about me, Tina. I've got the hang of this now. I think I'll keep going. I can hardly get lost, can I?'

'You'll probably meet Tom and Jack coming back,' Christina said, manoeuvring the sleigh in a wide arc as she started to make her way back.

Kat skated on, quite pleased with herself. The air was crisp and a pale winter sun was beaming down out of a cloudless blue sky. Far down on the ice she noticed an artist, busily recording the scene for posterity. Several other painters were seated on the bank, but this one had settled himself in the thick of things, sitting on a camp stool in front of his easel.

Perhaps he wouldn't mind if she stole a look at his work. Local people who came here on a regular basis were probably used to tourists taking an interest. He might even be one of those quick-sketch artists who tore their work off a pad as soon as it was finished, to sell to the nearest buyer. If she saw something that was cleverly done, but not too expensive, she might buy it as a present for Mum.

As she skated closer, she saw that the man was well-equipped with paints and other paraphernalia, obviously someone working on a more professional level than what she had been expecting. Just then, all at once, a group of youths, travelling at great speed, flashed by her, and one of them accidentally jogged her elbow.

'Sorry!' he shouted, looking back over his shoulder.

Caught off balance, Kat skidded sideways and crashed into the artist's easel. Paints, canvas and palette flew in all directions, as she landed in a heap beside the artist's stool. Winded and embarrassed, she gazed up into the furious eyes of Ambrose Legris!

'Not you again!' he snapped.

'You stole my line!' she cried, her brown eyes flashing. 'I am very, very sorry, Mr Legris, but it wasn't my fault.

Those boys crashed into me and there wasn't a thing I could do about it!'

He stopped to gather up his scattered belongings, muttering as he did so. Kat was thankful that her knowledge of French was rather shaky. To judge by the look on his face he was probably saying a lot of uncomplimentary things about her. She felt a sense of déja vu as she tried to get back on her feet.

'Aren't you going to help me up?' she demanded, but he didn't reply, displaying his customary lack of couth.

Fortunately two more young men came up behind her and helped her to her feet.

'What's the matter with you, mister?' one of them wanted to know. 'Can't you help a lady to her feet?'

Ambrose glared at him.

'Just get her away from me, before I lose my temper. Just look at this, a whole morning's work ruined, and this was a commission!'

'I've said I'm sorry,' Kat said weakly,

but he turned away to look at his canvas.

It didn't seem to be damaged, and she thought that he could probably save most of his work.

'Well, are you going to stand there all day staring at me?' Ambrose demanded, and Kat's rescuers took the hint.

Linking arms with her they sped off down the ice until she had to beg them to stop. After her fall she knew that she needed all her strength to get back, and her hip was aching where she had landed on hard ice. She would have bruises tomorrow.

There was still no sign of Tom and Jack, so, painfully, she made her way back to the spot where she had left Christina. Before she had gone very far she saw them skimming towards her. She hadn't realised that her sister was such a good skater, but then she had the handle of the sleigh to hold on to, which would help her to keep her balance.

'I think I'll have to go back to the

beginning and wait for you there,' she said, feeling very sorry for herself as she explained what had happened.

Christina didn't show her much sympathy.

'Everyone has a spill now and then,' she said. 'It goes with the territory. A nice hot bath will put you right.'

'But you should have heard Ambrose, Tina. He was so rude.'

'Yes, well, I don't suppose he was best pleased at having his work destroyed.'

'Nothing was destroyed, as you put it. Anyway, if he insists on sitting right in the line of traffic he must expect to run into trouble now and then.'

Christina laughed unkindly.

'You're just miffed because you keep making a bad impression on the so-attractive Ambrose Legris, little sister.'

Kat was forced to admit to herself that Christina might be right!

6

Rose Ingram was missing her daughter more than she cared to admit. She knew that Kat was coming back in a few weeks' time, but Canada seemed so far away. The weather outside was blustery and raw, just the right sort of day to work in the kitchen, in the comforting heat.

She decided to while away the time by turning out the store cupboard, a task which was long overdue. She would begin by emptying everything on to the kitchen table before giving the shelves a good scrub with soapy water, then she would throw out a few things that were past their sell-by date before rewarding herself with a nice cup of tea.

She was perched on a step stool, humming along with the radio, when Gyp got up from her bed and began to bark frantically. Rose's heart sank. Who on earth could be coming to the door at this hour of the morning? And here she was in a well-darned jumper and her head tied up in an old scarf! A glance out of the window made her spirits sink even lower as Nigel's car drew into the yard. Even worse, it was followed by an even more expensive-looking vehicle which did a sharp turn before coming to a stop beside Nigel, almost as if its owner was preparing for a quick getaway.

The door opened and Nigel burst into the kitchen, his face flushed with excitement.

'I've brought a prospective buyer to look over the property,' he announced.

'What?'

His mother paused in the act of freeing her curls from the faded scarf.

'What do you mean, you've brought a prospective buyer? I haven't decided to sell, Nigel. Surely you remember that?'

Nigel made a disgusted sound.

'Of course I remember, Mother. I told Mr Burstyn that, but surely there's no harm in letting him look around. If he makes an offer, you can come to a decision then. After all, it's possible that he may not like the place.'

Rose gave him a stern look.

'It simply isn't convenient for him to go over the house today, Nigel.'

Actually the house was fairly neat and tidy, apart from her unmade bed, but that wasn't the point. If anyone did come to view the place she would want time to prepare all the little touches that made a home look welcoming and saleable — a fire in the sitting-room, the scent of new-baked bread, flowers in the bedrooms. Well, potted plants, anyway, this being February.

'Oh, he's not interested in the house,' Nigel said. 'Look, I'm just going to take him around and I'll drop in afterwards and tell you all about it, all right?'

Watching from the window, Rose saw a burly man in green wellies and a padded jacket strolling off behind her son as they headed down to the stream which gave the farm its name. Still annoyed, she turned back to her task, although she no longer felt like working. Faced with the choice of washing down shelves or replacing everything, higgledy piggledy, she thought she'd better carry on. She snapped off the radio.

'They could at least have taken you with them,' she told Gyp, and collapsing into her basket by the stove, the dog grumbled an agreement.

Rose was puzzled. If the man was a prospective buyer, who didn't wish to view the house, what did he want? A small flicker of hope flared up. Perhaps he just wanted to buy the fields for some purpose. That might be the solution to their problems. While she would hate to see new bungalows springing up on the river bank, being able to stay on in her dear, old home would be wonderful.

Some time later, the men returned, and Mr Burstyn, or whatever his name was, got into his car and drove away.

'Well?'

Rose eyed her son with distaste. He hadn't even troubled to remove his boots before coming back indoors, although this had always been a firm rule on the farm. Surely Rosemary didn't allow him to track mud into their house, with its black and white floor tiles and white walls. Nigel followed her gaze down to his boots and got the message.

'Sorry, Mum, it's not worth taking them off. I'm not stopping. Just came in to say goodbye.'

'You're not going anywhere until you tell me what all that was about. Is this man interested in buying the fields? What did he say?'

Nigel hesitated.

'Better sit down, Mother.'

He pulled out a chair and sat down at the table.

'He's interested in buying the whole property, house and all.'

'But you said he isn't interested in the house. I don't understand.'

'Mr Burstyn is the head of a very

large business conglomerate in America, Mother. He wants to buy property within easy reach of London, to turn into an international conference centre. He wants a place in a district with pretty scenery and near to historic sites. Foreign businessmen will bring their wives with them, and while business is being transacted the ladies will be taken off to visit stately homes and gardens, that sort of thing.'

Rose seized on the words, stately home.

'Then why doesn't he just buy up a stately home and renovate that? His visitors would love to stay in a castle full of ghosts and suits of armour. Come to that, this house is hardly big enough for anything like a conference centre. I suppose he wants to put up lots of chalets in Long Meadow!'

'Oh, no. He means to bulldoze the house, of course, and build a modern hotel-type structure in its place, with a ballroom, and lots of sleeping accommodation with en suite bathrooms.'

Nigel was so wrapped up in his grandiose schemes that he failed to notice the glint in his mother's eye. It was a long time since she had let rip, as her family put it, but she could feel anger bubbling up inside her, ready to pour out like lava from a volcano.

'And it means nothing to you that this house that has been in the Ingram family for two hundred years, my home, I mind you, will be torn down?'

Her son shrugged.

'All good things must come to an end. You know quite well that the farm isn't paying its way any more. We really don't have much choice, do we? And I think we should snap up this offer right away, before Burstyn changes his mind. We may never get another one as good as this. The land isn't worth anywhere near what he's prepared to pay. No farmer would hand over that sort of money.'

'We? What is all this we, Nigel?'

He looked puzzled.

'Why, the four of us, of course, you,

me, Christina and Kat.'

'And you expect that if the farm is sold, the revenue will be split four ways?'

'Well, this place is our inheritance, isn't it? River Farm, in the Ingram family for two centuries or whatever it is.'

Rose said nothing, and then he took her breath away with his next statement.

'Actually, as I'm the eldest son, the only son, the old place should come to me when you're gone. As it is, I'm quite prepared to share it with the girls, if it's sold soon.'

'Actually,' Rose said, mimicking his words, 'actually River Farm now belongs to me. That is how I was provided for in your father's will, as well you know. I have the right to leave it to whomever I please, or to sell it, if that's what it all comes down to. The farm is mine, Nigel, mine. Is that clearly understood?'

As usual, her words rolled off him

like water off a duck's back.

'I'd better be on my way,' he said, glancing at his watch. 'Now, think this over, Mother, and don't leave it too long before you come to a decision. Of course, I suppose it won't hurt to keep him in suspense for a bit. Maybe he'll up the price a bit more if he gets anxious.'

Then Nigel was gone, slamming the door behind him.

There was no hope of doing anything constructive around the house now.

'Come on, Gyp,' Rose said, taking down her old tweed coat from its peg, and shrugging her arms into it.

She then pulled on her boots while the dog leaped up and down with excitement. Together they went out into the wind and hastened up the hill.

Standing there, looking down on the home she loved, Rose let a tear roll unheeded down her weatherbeaten face. If only Joe were here! But then, if he hadn't died, there would be no question of selling the place now. If only she had someone to talk to, somebody who would understand.

On the other side of the wood, George Logan was checking the fences on the boundary line, with Shep at his side. Suddenly the dog barked and an answering yelp came from not far away. Shep cleared the stile with one bound. George's heart leaped. Someone was out there with Gyp. Was Kat back already? He ran through the trees, stopping in disappointment when he found her mother leaning wearily against an enormous oak, in the lee of the wind.

'I thought you were Kat,' he said, coming to a halt.

'Sorry to disappoint you.' Rose smiled. 'Kat isn't due back until the end of the month. No it's just me. I've had some disturbing news, and I just had to come out and walk it off, if you know what I mean.'

George nodded. He had known Rose all his life, and she was as dear to him as if she was his real aunt, rather than the neighbour he had called Auntie Rose as a child.

'I thought I saw Nigel's car,' he began.

Rose nodded wryly.

'Yes, you did.'

'Want to talk about it? I mean, not if it's private or anything, but you look like you could use a shoulder to lean on.'

'I know Kat told you that we've had difficulty keeping things going since Joe died. I promised her I'd wait until she comes back from Canada before making a decision, but now Nigel has rather forced my hand. He turned up this morning, quite unannounced, bringing an American billionaire who wants to buy the place.'

George didn't know how to respond to this.

'This American wants to build some sort of international conference centre, which would mean pulling down the house and putting up some modern horror, all concrete and glass. I can't bear it, George! I've half come to terms with the fact that I might have to move away, but I did imagine that another family would come to live here, loving the dear old house and bringing up happy children there.'

'So what will you do?'

Rose wiped away a tear.

'I'll keep my promise to Kat, and discuss it with her when she comes home, but I'm very much afraid that I may have to give in. There doesn't seem to be any other solution.'

'I did propose a solution, Rose.'

She looked at him fondly.

'I know you did, dear, and I only wish it could come about, not just to save River Farm, I mean. Joe and I, well, we always hoped that you and Kat would end up together, but it seems that she has other ideas.'

'I'm afraid I'm a bit dull,' George said sadly. 'Kat thinks that love should be exciting, you see. She thinks of me as a brother, good old George from next door.'

'There's a lot to be said for companionship and trust in a marriage,' Rose said softly. 'When I first met my Joe I didn't feel as though I'd been hit by a bolt of lightning. I just felt safe with him, and knew I'd want him to be there for the rest of our lives. And he never gave me any reason to feel otherwise.'

'Yes, well, just try telling that to Kat.'

Rose patted him on the shoulder.

'Don't give up, George! Faint heart never won fair lady, as they say. But as for Kat wanting a bit of excitement, well, maybe you could do something wildly romantic to surprise her.'

He looked doubtful.

'Like sending her flowers, do you mean?'

'A little more than that, dear. Look, I'm beginning to get an idea!'

George listened with interest as Kat's mother began to talk. He bit his lip, wondering if there was anything in what she had to say. He knew that she was genuinely interested in bringing him and Kat together for good. Even though a marriage between them would help to solve Rose's problems, that fact had nothing to do with her willingness to see them as man and wife some day.

'And you really think it would work?' he asked when she had finished, his face alight with hope.

'Well, of course, I can't promise anything, George, but it's worth a try, isn't it? Play your cards right and Kat may well change her mind.'

'I'll go home right away and discuss it with Dad. I've finished checking the fences and I know just where he'll be on a day like this, tinkering with the tractor in the shed!'

He strode off, whistling. Rose watched him go. Gyp looked up into her face, as much as to say, what next?

'Yes, old girl, home we go!'

She set off down the hill, with the dog trotting in front of her. She very much hoped that it would all work out. She would love to have George for a son-in-law. In fact, and she pushed away the thought with a sense of shame, she wished that he was her son, rather than Nigel. Hard though she tried to understand her son, she blamed herself for the way he had turned out. Where had she gone wrong? Even as a small boy he had been self-centred, not a bit like his kindly, sensible father.

Now he seemed so completely wrapped up in himself that he just wanted to get his hands on his inheritance, as he put it. How did he imagine that she was going to manage on a fraction of what the sale of the farm might bring in? Why, she might live for another thirty years!

Oh, Joe, she thought, I just don't know what to do for the best.

7

'Oh, no, Christina, I just won't do it, and you simply can't make me!' Kat exploded.

'Nonsense!'

Christina looked at her younger sister in exasperation.

'It's only a dinner invitation. Surely the two of you can get along in a civilised manner for a couple of hours.'

Kat looked stubborn.

'Come on, Kat! I've already accepted the invitation and booked a sitter for the children. I'm rather looking forward to it, as it happens. I've only been in that house once or twice before, and never for a meal.'

'You and Tom go then. Cancel the babysitter and I'll stay here and hold the fort.'

'I won't hear of such a thing. Genevieve specifically invited you, Kat, because you're a visitor. It would be a real insult to refuse to go, and if Ambrose does dislike you as much as you think, wouldn't you be playing right into his hands by staying away? Don't be such a wimp.'

That stung.

'All right, I'll come, but if that man so much as looks at me sideways . . . '

'So far he's only had to look down,' Christina retorted. 'You always seem to be throwing yourself at his feet.'

Kat glared at her. She really didn't know if she could put up with Ambrose for a whole evening, but on the other hand she was curious to see how he and his sister lived. Well, she had never been one to turn down a challenge. She would put on her glad rags and try to reverse his earlier impression of her.

She toyed with the idea of going into Ottawa to buy something new and glamorous, but had to remind herself that she needed to conserve her dwindling resources. Besides, he hadn't seen her green dress. She would have to make do with that.

When the three of them drove up to the Legris house, every window was ablaze with light.

'I wouldn't like to have to pay their electricity bill,' Tom muttered, as they stood on the doorstep, waiting for someone to let them in.

'Shush!' Christina said as she dug her husband in the ribs. 'If anyone hears you, they'll think you're jealous.'

'Jealous my foot! Should I ring again? Maybe nobody heard the bell the first time.'

Kat could see why the neighbours might be envious of anyone who could afford a huge house like this. To think that Ambrose's great-grandfather had built this great barn of a place as a summer retreat! In that case, what must his Montreal house have been like?

'So sorry!'

Genevieve stood back from the door, waving them in.

'I was down in the wine cellar and didn't hear the bell.'

She was wearing a cashmere sweater in a deep shade of blue, over an ankle-length skirt of matching corduroy. Navy blue felt clogs completed her ensemble. She took their coats and boots, tucking them away in a walk-in closet. As she slipped on her indoor shoes, Kate looked around, trying not to appear impressed. The ceiling of the dark-panelled hall rose into a glass dome high above them. A crystal chandelier illuminated the magnificent staircase and the hall below. The upper rooms were reached by an open passageway which was a sort of long balcony affair with wrought iron railings enclosing the outer edge to prevent anyone from falling off.

'Come in by the fire,' Genevieve said. 'Ambrose shouldn't be long. He was still in the shower when I came downstairs.'

She led the way into a room, which was even more beautiful than the hall. A cheerful, log fire was burning in a stone fireplace which took up most of one wall, and floor-to-ceiling shelves were filled with books and pewter ornaments. Long wine-coloured velvet curtains completed the cosy decor. As Genevieve moved to close them, Kat saw that the deeply-recessed windows held cushioned window seats, just like the ones at River Farm. A wave of homesickness swept over her. How was Mum getting along, she wondered, three thousand miles away.

'Sorry to keep you waiting, folks!'

Ambrose swept into the room and went straight to the fire to warm his hands. Like his sister, he was wearing a cashmere top, and he had chosen corduroy trousers and sheepskin moccasins.

His eyes opened wide when he saw Kat, taking in her appearance from head to toe. She hated it when men assessed her like that, yet she was pleased to see that she was making an impression. Until now, apart from being bundled up in outdoor clothes, he had only seen her as an awful scruff, dressed in her babysitting outfit and covered in cat hair.

But if he draws attention to the fact that he hardly recognises me, he'll get the rough edge of my tongue, she thought. But he behaved like a perfect gentleman, asking her if she'd prefer sweet or dry sherry. Happily, she joined in the toast he proposed, to friends from far and near.

'Dinner is served, madame.'

A middle-aged woman, smartly dressed in a cap and apron, stood in the doorway, addressing Genevieve.

'Merci, Beatrice. Follow me, everyone.'

With a mocking bow, Ambrose turned to Kat.

'May I have the pleasure, mam'selle?'

He escorted her into the dining-room and pushed her chair into place behind her. Her glance took in the table, which was beautifully set with crystal and expensive dinnerware. To judge by the amount of cutlery on the table, they could expect to be served several courses!

Beatrice served the meal quietly and

effortlessly. As they progressed from pâté to vichyssoise, followed by roast lamb, Ambrose kept up a polite conversation, turning from Tom on his left to Kat at his right. She had to admit that he was the perfect host. Not to be outdone, Christina asked Genevieve what project she was currently working on.

'I have a new commission, a giant piece for the foyer of a government building. Perhaps you would care to see it later? And you, Kat, do you have an interest in such things?'

'I'd love to see your work,' Kat said diplomatically, although frankly, she was more interested in seeing Ambrose's paintings.

Christina had professed to be impressed by them, Tom was less so. She would like to judge for herself. Ambrose seemed to tune into her thoughts.

'And possibly you would like to see my latest work, also, mam'selle Kat? You would like to see what became of

80

the painting you so nearly destroyed on the Rideau Canal?'

Kat blushed, not knowing how to respond. Genevieve laughed.

'Don't worry about his silly painting. There are more where that one came from!'

This comment did little to put Kat at ease, but Tom came to her rescue.

'I've often wondered, Ambrose, why you work at your paintings right in the middle of things. Wouldn't a rough sketch do just as well, or a photograph, say, when you could work in the comfort of your own home, rather than freezing to death on the canal?'

'Ah, but I must soak up the atmosphere! I must be part of the scene, to experience it, to capture its soul!'

He waved an arm dramatically, almost sending Kat's wine glass flying. She managed to swallow a smile as she caught sight of her brother-in-law, raising his eyes to the ceiling. A-down-to-earth person, Tom had little patience with the artistic temperament, thinking it pretentious.

'This meal is absolutely delicious,' Kat told Genevieve, biting into a cream-filled meringue. 'Your cook is marvellous.'

'Oh, Beatrice isn't my cook,' Genevieve said casually. 'She and her partner, Agathe, run a superb catering business. I always hire them when we want to give a dinner party. If it was left to me to do the cooking you'd be eating macaroni.'

So Kat had been wrong. There were no servants in the Legris household after all. Of course, Genevieve could hardly keep up a house this size on her own. Even those intricately-carved banisters must take time to dust. Very likely they had a daily woman who came in from time to time.

'And now for the grand tour,' Ambrose told them. 'I'm going to show Kat my studio. Would the rest of you like to come along?'

'Later,' his sister told him. 'We'll go

back to the other room and have our coffee by the fire.'

Tom gave a slight frown, but good manners prevailed, and he followed their hostess out of the room.

'Will you be all right?' Christina mouthed and Kat nodded.

She was feeling more at ease with Ambrose now. She was seeing another side to him, smooth, sophisticated. She followed him down the hall and out through a small door into another passageway. They passed through a conservatory, filled with exotic plants, and into a room at the other end. Kat gasped with surprise. She found herself looking at a vast expanse of glass. One wall was nothing but a huge window. Tom's remark came back to her about what on earth it must cost to heat a room like this during the Canadian winter.

Paintings were stacked everywhere, on the floor, on easels, on top of a cupboard.

'So you do work here at times?' she

asked. 'You don't take up semi-permanent residence on the canal?'

He smiled, and despite herself, her heart turned over. Ambrose Legris was very attractive!

'Come, I'll show you some of the pieces which are about to be shipped to a gallery in Toronto. You are lucky. The woman who frames them will be here to pick them up tomorrow.'

He displayed several canvases in turn, and she was enchanted by the vibrant colours, the sense of life and movement. Some were street scenes, others had rural backgrounds, but every painting showed people and animals, playing busily, working or shopping. Kat particularly liked one of a country fair, where children were riding on a carousel or lining up to try their luck at the hoopla stall. She could see why his paintings commanded such high prices. They generated a happy feeling in the onlooker.

'They're wonderful, Ambrose! So full of life and energy!'

'I'm glad you like them.'

'What did you do with the one I knocked over on the canal? Were you able to save it?'

He smiled mockingly, and led the way to a small easel in the corner of the room. Whipping off the cloth which covered the painting displayed there, he stood back to watch her reaction. Kat gasped. In the forefront of the picture, a skater was sprawled on the ice, while two passers-by reached down to assist her.

'That's me!' she exclaimed.

'Your eyes are working well, mam'selle.'

'But how . . . '

'I simply painted over the little girls that I had already immortalised there, and inserted Kat Ingram instead. It has a certain charm, don't you think?'

'I can't think who would buy a picture of me, lying in a heap on the ice,' Kat said, feeling awkward. 'You told me it was a commission. Will it meet with the buyer's approval?'

'Oh, but I shall never part with this one. It will be a constant reminder of the little English miss who came into my life one winter and threw herself at my feet, twice!'

Kat was lost for words, and his next remark took her breath away.

'Perhaps we should celebrate the successful completion of the painting by going out on the town. Ottawa has some pleasant nightspots, or I might get tickets for the opera or the ballet. Where would you like to go?'

She didn't quite know how to reply to this. She would certainly like to go out with him, but nightclubs weren't really her scene.

8

'What were the paintings like?' Christina wanted to know once they had returned home, and Tom had gone to drive their babysitter back.

After checking on the children who were fast asleep in their beds, Christina had come back downstairs to make hot chocolate. The sisters were now sitting by the dying embers of the fire, sipping their drinks.

'Quite fascinating, really. As you told me, the man really does seem to know what he's doing.'

'I was quite annoyed when Ambrose took you off by yourself. I really wanted to see his work for myself, and I know that Tom was bored by Genevieve's blow-by-blow description of her tapestry work, beautiful though it is. In view of the fact that Ambrose has been treating you like something the cat brought in, I wouldn't have expected him to keep you all to himself.'

'He was quite pleasant, actually.'

'But I still don't see why . . . '

Kat did her best to look nonchalant.

'He wanted me to be the first to see the painting he did of me.'

'What?'

'You heard.'

Christina looked puzzled.

'But I don't understand. How could he paint a portrait of you when he's hardly seen you before tonight? Yours isn't exactly the face that launched a thousand ships, is it?'

'Thanks a heap!' Kat said with a grin, taking this sisterly remark for what it was worth.

'Actually, he didn't make too much of my face, more my bottom, really.'

Christina's horrified response was cut short by the reappearance of her husband, who came into the room, blowing on his fingers.

'Put another log on that fire, will you, Kat? I'm frozen. Mrs Mack dropped her house key in the snow and it took for ever to find it. I thought at one point that I'd have to break a window to get the woman inside. Any more of that cocoa?'

'In a minute, dear. Kat is about to tell us all about a portrait of her which Ambrose has painted.'

Tom looked at Kat with raised eyebrows and she recounted her surprise at seeing herself in oils for the first time.

'Perhaps I should make Legris an offer for the thing,' Tom teased. 'We'll put it up on my study wall with a label, Portrait of my Sister-in-Law. A fine conversation piece that would make.'

'Well, at least he's not cross with you any more for damaging the thing,' Christina said. 'They are our neighbours, after all. I wouldn't like there to be a coolness between us all over a silly thing like that.'

'Oh, he's not cross,' Kat said, with the air of one about to drop a bombshell. 'In fact, he's asked me out, on a date, no less.'

Christina's jaw dropped.

'Really? Where is he taking you?'

'I hope you said no,' Tom grumbled. 'I don't know what it is about that guy, but I wouldn't trust him further than I could throw him.'

'You don't like him because he's better-looking than you,' his wife teased, although in actual fact she thought that Tom could beat any dark-eyed Frenchman hands down when it came to appearance.

'It's not that, Tina. I know his sort. Women find him fascinating and then as soon as they fall for him he drops them, left, right and centre.'

'How can you say that, Tom? We've never seen any evidence of that, and anyway, Kat is a grown woman. She can take care of herself.'

'Excuse me!' Kat was getting annoyed. 'Do you have to talk about me as though I wasn't here? I don't see the harm in going out on a date with one of your neighbours. After all, I'll be heading back to England before long, so I'm hardly going to be led astray by Ambrose, fascinating or not!'

Yet a little voice inside her said that a little holiday romance with an attractive, sophisticated man might not be a bad thing. She had turned down his offer of an evening at the opera or the ballet. Those were things she could do in England. She was here to sample all that Canada had to offer, so she had told him that she would prefer to take part in some other winter activity, something she couldn't experience back home.

He had opened his eyes wide at that, reminding her that she had already tried cross-country skiing and outdoor skating, and had come to grief on both occasions. Still, she had insisted, and he replied that he would give it some thought and let her know.

'It won't be downhill skiing,' Tom mused. 'He must know you're not up to that. Curling, perhaps? Bob-sledding?'

'We'll just have to wait and see,' his

wife told him. 'Now, shouldn't we get to bed? You have to go to work in the morning, remember.'

And so they banked down the fire and said their good-nights.

Two days later, Kat came downstairs with her head in a towel.

'There was a phone call for you while you were in the bath,' Christina told her. 'Ambrose Legris, with plans for your date.'

'Oh! Am I supposed to call him back?'

'No, no. I took a message. You're only meant to call him if the arrangements don't suit you. He says you're to dress warmly and he'll pick you up at eight.'

'Did he say what he's got in mind?'

Christina looked put out.

'A sleigh ride, apparently. I do think he might have invited all of us. The children would have loved it.'

'What sort of sleigh ride?'

Kat had a bizarre mental picture of herself being towed along by Ambrose, hunched up on a tiny sleigh like the one her niece had ridden on the canal.

'Well, like the ones the church puts on for the Sunday School children, I suppose. A couple of the local farmers have these long, flat wagons on runners, which are pulled with horses or tractors. The kids sit on bales of hay and have a great time.'

Kat agreed that it would have been kinder to include the rest of the family, but she was secretly glad that she and Ambrose would be alone, that's if he didn't bring Genevieve along to play gooseberry! Seeing that her sister was feeling rather grumpy, Kat excused herself and went back upstairs to dry her hair. At least she wouldn't need to dress up for their date. Her ordinary jumper and trousers would be hidden by the parka and down-filled snow pants she had borrowed from Christina.

She resolved to spend the day entertaining Jack and Lucy, which would give their mother a break. Even Cinderella hadn't sat around all day, waiting for the glass coach to arrive! She had better pull her weight while Christina got on with the household chores.

But Kat was waiting at the window, long before eight o'clock.

'What you looking at, Auntie? Is it a fire truck?' her nephew asked.

'Let's hope not,' she told him, and he looked disappointed.

He was at the stage where he wanted to be a fireman when he grew up. Last week it had been a doctor, after he had been to get his vaccination booster. Next week it would probably be something else. His eyes opened wide with excitement when they heard the sound of horses' hooves and the jangling of bells.

'Mommy, Mommy, is it Santa Claus?'

'No, darling. Santa has gone back to the North Pole now. He has to help the elves to make all the toys to give to good little girls and boys next Christmas. Let me get to the window and have a look.'

The children had their noses pressed to the window as Ambrose drew his horse to a halt in front of the house. It was a beautiful black mare wearing scarlet harness, and as for the sleigh, it was not the farm wagon that Christina had described, but a beautiful little red cutter, with a high back and sides.

'It's just like the one on the Christmas card you sent us,' Kat breathed.

'Is Santa, is Santa!' Lucy babbled, jumping up and down.

'No, darling. I know it looks like the sleigh in your story book, but the man doesn't have a red suit, does he?'

Lucy pouted.

'Want presents,' she muttered.

'Now we know why the rest of you weren't invited,' Kat remarked. 'That thing only seats two, by the look of it.'

'For goodness' sake, stop dithering and get out there,' Christina told her. 'It's obvious that the man isn't going to come to the door to fetch you, and he won't want to keep the horse standing on a cold night like this.'

Hastily cramming her woollen hat over her hair, Kat hurried outside. Ambrose helped her up into the sleigh and they were off, waving gaily to the group at the window.

'Pull that bearskin over you,' Ambrose ordered, indicating a large, fur rug. 'And before you tell me that fur is politically incorrect, let me tell you that this one dates from my great grandfather's time, when everyone used them. Refusing to use it won't bring back an animal that has been dead for almost one hundred years.'

Kat snuggled down under the fur, saying nothing. As they moved down the quiet streets, to the tune of sleigh bells, which were attached in rows to narrow leather straps, she felt herself transported back in time, to an era when Canadians always travelled like this in winter. Nowadays, there were mechanised snow ploughs to keep the streets clear, but long ago people had to put up with several feet of snow which lasted for five months or more.

'Where are we going, Ambrose?'

'Back to my place. We have trails cut through the bush where we exercise the horses in all seasons, cherie.'

He had called her cherie! Was the endearment just a slip of the tongue, or was it meant? Filled with happiness she pulled her hat down over her ears and prepared to enjoy the outing.

'I wanted you to meet Belle,' Ambrose said, as he urged them into a trot.

The beautiful animal tossed her head and snorted. Kat wondered if she was used for anything else besides pulling a sleigh. It was too heavy for riding and it was unlikely that Ambrose or his sister went on this sort of outing very often. Perhaps he had a whole string of girlfriends whom he took out to the woods on winter evenings!

The ride was an enchanting experience. They went along what seemed to be endless trails through the bush, with the wind sighing softly in the tall pines.

Looking up, Kat saw the sky filled with stars around a pale moon. She gave a sigh of pleasure and her breath came out in a white cloud. Although it was a frosty night she felt snug and comfortable under the bearskin rug and she was acutely aware of Ambrose, sitting close beside her. The ride in this little cutter was light years away from the church sleigh ride that Christina had described to her. There was a sense of intimacy about it.

She soon lost track of time, but even so, the ride came to an end all too soon. She would have liked it to go on for ever. However, they emerged from the bush and approached the house. The horse quickened its pace as they came into the stable yard, where an elderly man came out to take charge of her.

'Come in and see the other horses,' Ambrose said, 'and then I'll run you home in the car.'

Kat had been wondering if he would invite her into the house, and if so, how could she frame a polite refusal without giving offence? So how was it that she now felt a keen sense of disappointment? Still, there might be other evenings. Two more horses looked up with interest as the older man, referred to by Ambrose as Maurice, led their stable mate into the building and began to rub her down. These other animals were riding horses, used by Ambrose and his sister.

'Do you ride, Kat?'

'Oh, yes,' she replied, thinking of old Polly, her beloved pony, who was spending her last days in peace at River Farm.

What would happen to poor Polly if the farm had to be sold? She pushed the thought from her, unwilling to let her worries spoil the evening.

The drive back to the Fryes' house took no time at all.

'I'll see you to the door,' Ambrose said, and when they reached the step he took her into his arms and gave her a lingering kiss.

Kat responded eagerly, but in putting

her arms around him she inadvertently leaned on the doorbell and the sound echoed through the house.

'Someone's coming,' she hissed, struggling to free herself from his embrace, but he only laughed, and hugged her more tightly.

The door flew open. Was she dreaming? Kat could not believe her eyes!

'George!' she said weakly.

'Hello, Kat,' the vision said, eyeing Ambrose with hostility.

'Good-night, cherie,' Ambrose said, in that mocking way of his, as he dashed back to his car, leaving Kat standing on the doorstep, puzzled and embarrassed.

9

After speaking to Rose the day they had met, George Logan had rushed home, fired with enthusiasm. He had loved Kat for a long time but his proposal of marriage had met with a firm refusal. She hadn't even taken him seriously, suggesting that it was made in the light-hearted banter they'd engaged in for years. He'd phrased it all wrong — it's too bad you're in danger of losing the farm. Marry me and it will solve all your problems!

He could have bitten his tongue out as soon as he'd said it. Girls wanted a bit of romance, didn't they? He should have taken Kat out on the town and proposed in some romantic setting, over white wine, with soft music in the background. And what had he done instead? Blurted everything out on a rainswept hillside, with the two of them standing there in muddy boots! Kat had turned him down gently, insisting that she thought of him as a brother. She wasn't in love with him.

He still had the faint hope that those feelings could change in time, if he made more of an effort to woo her, as his grandmother would have put it. He realised now that companionable outings to the livestock sales left something to be desired in the romance department! But time was the one thing he didn't have. Kat had gone to Canada on the spur of the moment, and when she came back, decisions had to be made. Unless there was some sort of miracle, she and her mother would move away, very probably to some place out of reach. If Kat returned to London, that would be that. Farmers couldn't go haring off to the big city to wine and dine their girlfriends, could they?

He had poured out his heart to Rose, and she had been encouraging.

'You mustn't give up hope, dear. If I

were you, I wouldn't say anything more about marrying Kat in order to save River. Much as I appreciate the kind thought, it does sound rather like a business arrangement. You've got to convince her that you're really in love with her, farm or no farm.'

'But she thinks I'm dull,' George muttered.

'What you need is a bit of self-confidence, my lad. Just you listen to me. Kat is abroad at the moment. What can you do in the way of a romantic gesture?'

'Bombard her with letters? Send chocolates? I don't know. What else can I do from this distance?'

'Hop on a plane and go over there,' Rose said triumphantly.

'Hop on a plane!'

'That's what I said. Give Christina a call and invite yourself to stay. She'll be thrilled to see you again, I'm sure. Tell her to keep it a surprise from Kat and when you arrive, tell Kat you couldn't bear to spend another minute without her, something like that. What could be more romantic?'

It was madness, of course, but the more he thought about it, the more he realised that it could work. If only Dad would lend him the money. Fortunately, his father was amused. He had always been fond of Kat, and would welcome her as a daughter-in-law. He also admired Rose, thinking of her as a gallant woman, struggling to carry on the work of the farm after the death of her husband, his best friend, Joe.

Then, too, he felt that it was high time that George was married and settled down.

'I daresay we can manage without you,' he said, sucking on his faithful old pipe. 'Lucky for you you didn't decide to rush off during our busy time, and I can manage to rustle up the plane fare. Mind, I'll expect you to work twice as hard to make up for it after you get back!'

He laughed heartily.

As Rose had forecast, Christina was

delighted to hear from him.

'Certainly we can put you up for a few nights, George. Kat is in the spare bedroom but we have a pull-out settee downstairs which has a very comfortable mattress. You can have that. Kat will get the surprise of her life when you get here. I shan't tell the children, of course, or young Jack will spill the beans. When are you coming? I hope you can get a flight at short notice.'

Unfortunately there was no flight available, so George agreed to go on standby, which was no bad thing in a way because he could get his ticket at a reduced price. After a wait of several hours at the airport, during which he drank endless cups of coffee and read a paperback thriller without taking in a word, he managed to catch a flight for Toronto.

After a train journey, which took almost as long as the flight from England, he arrived in Ottawa, to be met by Tom. He could have taken a connecting flight which would have had him there in half an hour, but that would have cost money and he wanted to save his cash to take Kat out and about.

He received a great welcome at the Fryes' home and settled down to wait for Kat, who was out for the evening with a neighbour, Christina explained.

Christina suggested that he might like to lie down after his exhausting journey, but he was too keyed up to sleep and opted instead to watch a hockey game on television with Tom. It was eleven o'clock before they heard a car stopping outside, and he was on his feet at once. Then, as the doorbell rang, he bounded to the front door and flung it open, hoping to pull Kat into his arms.

It was then that all his dreams came crashing down. Kat was in the arms of another man, and apparently happy to be there. What was more, he observed bitterly, the stranger seemed to be everything that he, George, was not — devastatingly handsome, with a

French accent that would bowl over any woman. Rich, too, by the look of it, George guessed — that car had cost a pretty penny.

'For goodness' sake, you two! Come in and shut the door. You're letting a wicked draught in here.'

Christina bustled into the hall, realising what had happened. George was standing there awkwardly, with a look on his face like a sick puppy while Kate, red-faced, was bending over to remove her snow boots.

'Isn't this a wonderful surprise?' Christina said brightly. 'George has come all the way from England to be with you.'

'Well, I didn't think he'd come from the North Pole!' Kat retorted, and her sister sighed.

If Kat was going to be difficult, they could look forward to a chilly atmosphere over the next few days, and she wasn't thinking about the weather!

'I think, if you don't mind, that I will take up your kind offer of a bed now,'

George said quietly. 'I'm suddenly feeling quite tired.'

The next morning, Kat and George behaved towards each other like polite strangers. Kat busied herself spooning oatmeal into Lucy's greedy little mouth, and George's attention was taken by young Jack, who insisted on bringing his whole collection of toy cars to show this new uncle.

Fat chance of me ever becoming the lad's uncle, George thought gloomily. The scene that he had played over and over in his mind during the long journey to Canada was very different to what had actually happened. Kat was supposed to have been overwhelmed by his sudden appearance and declaration of undying love, but instead of that she was acting as if she'd never seen him before. Where had it all gone wrong?

He knew the answer to that, of course. It was all to do with this Ambrose, or whatever his name was. Had Kat fallen in love with the fellow? How far had their relationship gone?

He suddenly felt sick with worry. Unable to eat another mouthful, he pushed his plate away, and cleared his throat.

'Kat?'

'Yes?'

Busily removing Lucy's bib and picking up the empty bowl, she didn't spare him a glance.

'It's about the man you were with last night,' he began. 'Are you . . . I mean, is there something more between you than just a good-night kiss? I have to know, Kat.'

She swung round furiously.

'I don't know what it has to do with you, George Logan! You turn up here, asking personal questions, and expect to get a civil answer. You don't own me, you know!'

She flounced out of the room and George's heart sank. Was this her way of telling him that she had really fallen for this Ambrose Legris?

10

'Can I have a word with you?' Christina asked her sister as she joined Kat later.

Kat looked up from the doll she was dressing for Lucy.

'Of course. What was it you wanted to say?'

Christina jerked a thumb towards the stairs.

'In private, please!'

Unwillingly, Kat followed her into the master bedroom. She could guess what was coming next — a telling-off about her attitude towards George.

Christina plumped up the pillows and crossly jerked the duvet into place.

'Now look here, Kat Ingram, this can't go on! Poor George has come all this way to be with you, and you can't even look him in the eye. He's moping around the house like a moonstruck calf, so what I want to know is, what do you intend to do about it?'

'I didn't ask him to come,' Kat muttered.

'No, you didn't, but he's here now, and that's what we have to deal with. Besides, it's so romantic. He tells me he's been in love with you for years, but you, fool that you are, only see him as a brother figure. He wanted you to see him in a different light, away from the farm, which is why he scraped a few pennies together and rushed over here to show you how much he cares. Isn't that worth something?'

'I suppose so,' Kat replied grudgingly.

'But it still doesn't cut any ice with you, is that it?'

Kat shrugged.

'Oh, I don't know. It doesn't seem to fit into the picture, that's all. Here I am, having a lovely holiday and I want to enjoy it to the full. Everything is so different here, Tina. I have to go back soon, and face all my problems, but in the meantime seeing something of

Ambrose Legris is doing me the world of good, lifting me out of myself, you know?'

Christina gave her an old-fashioned look, and Kat almost laughed. She looked so much like her mother, when she used to catch them lazing about instead of getting on with their homework or completing their farm chores.

'I do understand, Kat, but we have to face facts. George is here now, and even if you still don't want to marry him, you must at least spend some time with him. When do you think he last had a holiday?'

'I don't remember,' Kat said, wiping away a tear that threatened to run down her cheek.

'Exactly!' Christina went in for the kill. 'And he told me he had to borrow the money to come here. What do you think about that, my girl?'

'Emotional blackmail!'

'I don't care what you call it. You are going to do the right thing. Get up off that chair and go down and plan an outing with George. You can take a bus into Ottawa and see the sights.'

Christina was right, of course. George hadn't come all this way just to sit in the house talking to two toddlers. Shrieks of laughter floated up the stairs. He was pretending to be a bear, crawling round the floor and growling. Jack and Lucy loved him.

He looked up hopefully as the two girls came downstairs.

'Kat was just thinking that the two of you could go into Ottawa and see the sights,' Christina said firmly.

George's face brightened. He very much doubted that Kat had said any such thing, but he was grateful to her sister for making it happen. Now he'd be able to get Kat on her own for a few hours, and who knew how things might turn out?

George was surprised to find that, for the capital of Canada, Ottawa was quite a small city compared with London and Paris, places he had visited in the past.

Most of the things that Kat wanted to show him were within walking distance of Parliament Hill, although some of the Winterlude activities were held at more distant locations.

They walked down Wellington Street, and gazed at the Parliament buildings. The wide expanse of ground in front of the buildings was snow covered now, but, as Kat explained, there were lawns there where the ceremony of the Changing of the Guard was held on summer mornings for the delight of tourists.

'It must be lovely here at other times of the year,' she went on. 'Christina tells me they have a tulip festival here in the spring, with literally millions of tulips blooming all over the city. And now for the canal,' she said, and headed off.

Although it was the middle of the week, there were numerous people on the ice, joyfully racing up and down. George watched them with interest.

'And is this skating rink really five

miles long? This is incredible!'

'Want to have a go? We could hire skates.'

'No, thanks,' George said hastily. 'I won't be much use to Dad if I go home with a broken leg. It's interesting to watch, though! Did you see that old lady scooting about down there? She must be at least ninety. I can't think how she does it.'

'She's probably been skating since she was a toddler.' Kat laughed. 'Out here, they all seem to be put on skates and skis at an early age. Young Jack is already quite good, and Tom says that he'll probably start playing in a hockey team next year. That's ice hockey, of course. You know how little boys at home always want footballs and boots for Christmas. Here it's skates and hockey sticks. I'd love to come back here in the summer,' she mused, turning to look back the way they had come. 'The pavements round here are full of stalls where they sell jewellery and bunches of flowers and hot dogs and cold drinks. You can take boat tours on the canal. Hard to imagine, isn't it? And, oh, George, guess what? They have a whole fleet of British double-decker buses that take tourists on sight-seeing tours around the city. Isn't that quaint? Yes, I'd love to be here in the warm weather.'

George almost told her that it would be a lovely place to come for a honeymoon, but he bit back the words in time. No point in risking a further rebuff.

Instead he said, 'All this talk of hot dogs is making me hungry! When can we eat?'

Laughing, they set off and found a restaurant which didn't look too expensive. They ordered hot chicken sandwiches. When their meal arrived, George stared at his plate in disbelief. There was a huge sandwich, smothered in gravy, accompanied by an enormous pile of chips, a tub of coleslaw and a dill pickle.

'I gave you extra French fries, sir,' the

waitress whispered as he smiled his thanks.

Probably expecting a big tip, Kat thought. She hoped that George could afford it. He didn't seem to be too flush with spending money. She mentally reviewed the contents of her own slender purse. She did have her credit card with her, of course, but she reminded herself that she was unemployed, and it would be foolish to run up a bill she could not afford to repay.

'So what do you think of Canada?' George asked, as they worked their way through their lunch.

'I like it a lot, not that I've seen much of it yet. There's only so much one can do in a month. As I said, I'd like to be here in summer, when so much activity seems to centre around the lakes and the countryside. They have a place called Upper Canada Village where you can go to see how people lived years ago. Just think, George, they've taken various old houses and shops, and even a school, from other parts of Ontario and set them up there so it's just like going back in time.'

George saw his opening, and took it.

'Now there's an idea for the Ingrams! You already have a lovely old house. Now all you have to do is set up thatched cottages and things and River Farm could become a tourist attraction in its own right.'

Kat laughed.

'So we could, if we had a million pounds or so to help us get started. And, don't forget, if we did have a million we wouldn't be in difficulty now.'

George reached over and took her hand in his.

'Kat, dear, there's something you should know. I spoke to your mother just before we came away and . . . '

A look of alarm crossed Kat's lovely face.

'Mum's not ill, is she? Did she send you over here to break the news to me?'

'No, no, nothing like that. It's something that will come as a shock to you, though. There's been an offer for River Farm. An American billionaire wants to buy it and turn it into some kind of conference centre for international businessmen. He wants to bulldoze the house and build something else in its place.'

Kat blinked back the hot tears which threatened.

'How on earth did he pick on River Farm? It's a gorgeous place, of course, but there are far more scenic spots in England.'

'Nigel.'

'What?'

'Apparently your brother heard somehow that this man was looking for a suitable location, and persuaded him to look at the place. The chap has made a very generous offer, and Nigel thinks that he may go even higher if your mother keeps him waiting for a decision. It seems he's the sort of man who doesn't like to be thwarted. Once he's made up his mind about something he'll move heaven and earth to get what he wants.'

Kat was silent for a while, toying with her food.

'Here, are you all right?'

She saw George looking at her anxiously.

'Not exactly. This has come as an awful shock. What has Mum decided to do? Did she say?'

'As far as I know she's reserving judgment until you get back.'

'I don't see why. It's up to Mum, really. I mean, we're all grown up now, and I don't know how long she can soldier on alone, especially as poor old Simon is getting on. He'll keel over some day, and then where will we be? If this American really is willing to pay a good price, perhaps it's all for the best. Mum will have a nice little nest egg to fall back on.'

'That's another thing.'

George hesitated. Better go carefully here. He didn't think much of Nigel, but he was Kat's brother, after all, and blood is thicker than water.

'Nigel believes that the money should be divided up among all four of you,' he said at last.

'He would! Well, obviously the thing to do is for me to discuss this with Tom and Christina, and see what they think. Then we can let Mum know our views, although of course the final say should be hers. I tell you this, though, George. I couldn't bear to go back and see the dear old place in ruins. Apart from Mum, I have no other ties in England. If River Farm is sold, I'll stay here, in Canada. Tom and Christina will sponsor me, I'm sure.'

'I don't think it works that way any more,' George said gently. 'I'm sure you'd have to return to England first and apply to emigrate from there.'

'It's something to investigate, anyhow. Now, have you finished? If you have, I think we should go. There appears to be a queue over there, of people waiting to sit down.'

George spent the rest of the day in a state of misery. Matters were not improved when they passed a small art gallery offering pictures for sale. There was just one canvas in the window, propped up on a short-legged easel against a background of dark green velvet drapes.

'Why, it's one of Ambrose's pieces!' Kat cried, her eyes lighting up.

George stared at it gloomily. It was certainly well done, if you liked that sort of thing, a woman hanging out a line of colourful washing, which flapped on the breeze. A baby was sitting on the grass, laughing, as he blew the seeds off a dandelion clock. He supposed that this Legris chap had talent, but it didn't seem fair that he was independently wealthy as well.

He wondered if Kat was in love with the man. If so, he, George, had come all this way for nothing. And, if River Farm was sold, Kat would probably come back here, within easy reach of his rival. Not only that, the peaceful district where his own future lay would be altered irrevocably, with hordes of foreigners roaring past in fast cars, frightening the livestock.

He brightened suddenly, remembering that he still had a card up his sleeve. It was a long shot, of course, but there was still hope. Ignoring Kat's puzzled glance, he began to whistle under his breath.

11

'It's for you, Kat,' Christina called when she came back from answering the phone, holding Lucy on one hip.

Kat struggled out of her low armchair, trying not to look pleased. It must be Ambrose. Who else would be calling her here? Her mouth was dry as she picked up the receiver.

'Hello?'

'Hi, Kat. I was thinking that you might like to go out with me tomorrow evening.'

'Go out?'

'Yes, Mam'selle Echo, go out. How would you like to eat dinner and go dancing at the Chateau Laurier?'

Would Cinderella like to go to the ball?

'Well, yes, I'd love to,' she stammered, 'but can I get back to you on that? Tom and Christina might have something planned for me.'

'Or perhaps the faithful yokel?' he said mockingly.

'I'll call you later,' she said firmly, and put the phone down.

She was not about to have George sneered at, but nevertheless his presence did pose a problem.

'What did Ambrose want?' Christina asked casually, carefully not looking at George.

'He's invited me to have dinner and go dancing at the Chateau Laurier tomorrow evening. Isn't that the fairy-tale hotel near the canal, the one with the towers and the copper roof?'

'That's right. Very swish. And are you going?'

'I said I'd let him know. Perhaps you and Tom have plans for me.'

'No, but perhaps George has something in mind.'

The sisters looked at George, who shook his head. Christina had advised him to play it cool in case, in the tradition of the best romantic novels, he drove Kat straight into the arms of his rival by showing a too proprietary interest. But playing it cool was the last thing he felt like doing. What he really wanted to do was to land a satisfactory punch on the other chap's nose! However, he himself had no claim on Kat, more the pity, and she had a perfect right to go out with whomever she chose.

'Well, then, perhaps I'll go,' Kat said, looking pleased.

The thought of drifting around in the arms of the fascinating French artist while soft music played was delightful.

'But what am I going to wear?' she mourned. 'Ambrose has already seen me in that green dress.'

'Now isn't that too bad!' George muttered under his breath, but nobody heard him.

Kat and Christina were already halfway up the stairs.

'I've got just the thing, Kat. The dream of a dress. I bought it for Tom's staff party at Christmas, and I've only worn it once. It's a good thing we're the same size.'

Holding up the gorgeous midnight blue, chiffon-covered dress in front of her as she gazed into Christina's full-length mirror, Kat indulged in a pleasant little fantasy. Ambrose would look into her eyes and say — what? She came down to earth with a bump as Christina stepped forward with a cluck of annoyance.

'That hem is coming down. I'll have to put a stitch in it before you can wear it. No, don't you dare touch, Jack! Your hands are all sticky!'

When Kat came downstairs, all dressed up, ready to go, the men stared at her with undisguised admiration. Christina had helped her with her hair, which was piled up on top of her head, with several long tendrils hanging down. Her tweed coat rather spoiled the effect. By rights, she should have had furs or a dashing cape, but she had to make do with what she had. In any case, she was strongly opposed to animals being killed for their fur so that women could be wrapped in luxury.

At the chateau she couldn't help comparing her surroundings with the last restaurant meal she had shared with George. The two places were only half a mile away from each other, and yet they were light years apart. Here there were soft lights and music played by a three-piece ensemble. The waiters were smartly dressed and tables were set with linen and good quality dinnerware.

'Are you ready to order, sir?'

Ambrose looked up at the waiter and asked to see the wine list.

'Certainly, sir. One moment, sir.'

'What are you having, Kat?'

Ambrose looked at her enquiringly while the waiter was away.

'I want to choose the perfect wines to go with our meal.'

Kat was impressed. She was a little alarmed because her menu had no prices listed. Presumably they were printed on the menu which Ambrose had been given. She stifled a giggle. Nowadays it was quite normal for a woman to do the paying when she went out to dinner with a man. How would she have handled it if that had been the case tonight? Would she have snatched the menu from her escort saying, 'I'll take that!'

Oh, well, Ambrose wouldn't have brought her here if he couldn't afford it, so she might as well go mad! She asked for an orange and watercress vinaigrette, to be followed by pork medallions which, she understood, would be accompanied by steamed rice and baby carrots.

'It is such a pity that you must return to England in ten days' time,' Ambrose remarked. 'There is so much of Canada that I should like to show you.'

'That's very kind, but I'm lucky to have had such a lovely, long holiday as it is. Almost a month abroad!'

'Ah, yes, you must get back to your job, I suppose. Me, I could not imagine being tied down so, getting up early on a cold, winter morning and going out to battle the rush-hour traffic.'

Kat bit back a sharp retort. Not all of us has a private income to fall back on, she wanted to say. Like thousands of others, she herself knew what it was like to go to work on those frosty mornings, when a cosy bed beckoned and the spectre of an irate boss filled the mind as one struggled not to be late.

'As a matter of fact, I shall have to go job hunting as soon as I get back,' she said. 'Unfortunately I was made redundant last month which is why I'm able to take this vacation now.'

Ambrose spread his hands with the air of one who had seen a problem solved.

'Then of course you must stay longer, Kat. Stay until spring. Stay until summer. Never return at all!'

She laughed at this enthusiasm.

'No, Ambrose, I'm afraid I must go back as planned. My mother is expecting me, you see.'

She went on to confide in him about

the threat to her old home.

'But I do not see what the difficulty is. This rich man buys your farm and with the money your maman purchases a little house. She is happy. She no longer has to get up on a cold morning to feed the animals, and without the worry of what is to happen next, you will be free to lead your own life.'

Kat sighed.

'If only it were that simple.'

'But of course it is. You were not meant to be a farm girl, cherie. Here you sit in your lovely dress, with the candlelight casting shadows on your beautiful hair. You were made for better things.'

Kat was spared the need to make a response to this flattery because of a gale of applause coming from a nearby table. It was obviously some sort of family celebration because there were twelve people there, clapping as a beaming waiter came forward with a beautifully-decorated cake, bearing golden ornaments. One of the men stood up, proposing a toast.

'To Mum and Dad, and may the next fifty years be happy ones!' he said and the others in the group raised their glasses and echoed, 'To Mum and Dad!'

The smiling couple at the end of the table were their parents, then, celebrating a golden anniversary.

The son who had proposed the toast raised his eyebrows and lifted one finger in what was obviously a pre-arranged signal, for the orchestra immediately struck up a rendition of, 'Oh, how we danced, on the night we were wed' which happened to be a favourite tune of Kat's.

The elderly groom stood up and bowed to his wife, who got up, smiling. With great dignity they waltzed in the wide space between the tables and then they stopped to beckon to the rest of the diners to join them.

'Shall we?'

Without waiting for an answer, Ambrose took Kat's hand and led her into the centre of the floor. The orchestra repeated the requested piece, and then went into a series of other romantic tunes. Ambrose was a superb dancer. Although Kat was not as practised at it as he was, their steps matched perfectly.

Ambrose was much taller than Kat and when he pulled her closer to him her head rested just below his chin. She felt him softly kissing her hair as she drifted along with the music, in a state of bliss. The next piece was another favourite, and she felt that this was indeed a magical time in her life. River Farm and all her worries seemed far away.

They went back to their table for coffee, which did nothing to break Kat's mood. She wondered what it was like to be so wealthy that one enjoyed such outings as a matter of course. Part of her pleasure stemmed from the fact that such outings had, until now, been so rare in her life that she could count them on the fingers of one hand. On balance, she thought she preferred it that way. When such treats did come along, they were all the more enjoyable because of their rarity.

The evening came to an end all too soon, and she found herself on Christina's doorstep, melting into Ambrose's arms as he kissed her goodnight, murmuring endearments. This time it was her sister who came to open the door to her.

Inside, Tom was sprawled on the couch, watching an American sitcom.

'Have a good time, did you?' he enquired, without much interest.

'Lovely, thanks.'

She followed Christina into the kitchen.

'Where's George, then? Gone to bed already, has he?'

Christina turned a worried face in her direction.

'George has gone, Kat. He left this evening. Tom drove him to the station.'

Kat stared at her sister in amazement.

'What do you mean, gone? Gone where?'

'Home, I suppose. He was heading for Toronto, or so he said. He flew into Pearson Airport, so I guess he'll be flying out the same way.'

Kat sank down on a kitchen chair, all the wind taken out of her sails.

'But why, Christina?'

Her sister looked exasperated.

'Why do you think, Kat? The poor chap came all this way to be with you and you've hardly given him a moment of your time. No wonder he got fed up and decided to cut his losses.'

12

Next evening, Kat was in charge of the house. Tom and Christina had gone into Ottawa to see a newly-released movie.

'Are you sure you don't mind?' Christina had pleaded. 'It's just that Tom and I don't often get the chance to go out.'

'Of course not. You're giving me a lovely holiday here. I'm glad to be able to do something in return.'

So off they went, very much looking forward to the outing. Kat had put the children to bed, had read several stories to them, and dealt with requests for drinks of water. She had looked under Jack's bed and peered into his clothes closet, ready to do battle with possible monsters.

'See my bed, too,' little Lucy said, and Kat obliged, although anyone could see that there was nothing but a fallen doll under the child's crib, the legs of which were high off the floor.

Finally, Kat was downstairs by the fire, wondering whether to watch television or to tackle a jigsaw puzzle of Niagara Falls, which Christina had received for Christmas. Possibly she could do both at the same time. Anything to take her mind off what was troubling her. She felt so guilty about George.

'And so you should!' Christina had said sternly, when Kat had reached home after her evening out with Ambrose and found that George had gone.

In vain Kat had pleaded that it wasn't really her fault. She'd had nothing to do with George's appearance the week before, and as she kept saying, she had no commitment to him, so what was so wrong about going out with Ambrose?

'Under the circumstances you should have turned him down and gone out and about with George,' Christina had said.

Kat's only ally was Tom, who did at least try to see her point of view, even if he didn't care too much for Ambrose. So there it was. She realised that she had some hard thinking to do. Ambrose had casually mentioned the possibility of her locating in Canada for good, and he seemed to be saying that if that happened their relationship would continue.

As things stood she had to go back to England, at least to stand by Mum, but it was tempting to think that she might make Canada her permanent home. With her office skills, she could most likely find a job to do. A lot would depend on what Ambrose might say before she left. Was he in love with her? It seemed as if he might be, yet he hadn't put anything into words.

The doorbell rang, making her jump. Cautiously, she made her way to the door and squinted through the peephole. To her surprise it was Genevieve Legris. A small red sports car stood at the kerb, and there was no sign of Ambrose. His sister had obviously come alone.

'I'm so sorry, I'm afraid you've missed Christina,' Kat said, as she led the way into the living-room. 'She and Tom have gone into town to see a movie.'

'Oh, that's all right. It's you I wanted to see,' Genevieve said. 'In fact, it's just as well the others are not at home. What I have to say is rather private.'

'Oh?'

This sounded ominous. The other girl's blank expression gave nothing away.

'It is Ambrose, of course,' Genevieve said. 'You may have got the wrong impression, I think. You have been seeing rather a lot of him?'

'He has been kind enough to take me out once or twice, yes,' Kat admitted.

'And I suppose you are foolish enough to consider yourself in love with him after seeing how we live. Many women have fallen into the same trap and, yes, if I were not his sister I think that I should admire him very much also. He is an attractive man, and a rich one.'

Kat mentally counted to ten.

'I don't think it's any of your business if Ambrose takes me out, Genevieve. We're both over twenty-one and what's more, I'm aware that this can't last much longer. I'm due to return to England next week, and after that I doubt if I shall ever see your brother again.'

Genevieve gazed into the flames.

'I do not think that you know my brother at all, Kat. He is quite capable of chartering a plane to call on you at your home in England, and before you leave he will most likely try to make you believe that you are the only woman in the world for him. I have seen it all before.'

Kat decided that this conversation had gone far enough.

'Thank you for your concern, Genevieve, but I'm quite capable of taking care of myself, I assure you.'

Genevieve shrugged.

'Very well, have it your way. When your little house of cards comes tumbling down, do not say I failed to warn you. But when he comes to you to tell you of his undying love, ask him this. What of Marie-Angele, Ambrose Legris, what of Marie-Angele?'

'Who is Marie-Angele?' Kat asked, but Genevieve only stood up and wrapped her coat more tightly around her.

She let herself out, closing the front door with a bang, and moments later Kat heard the car drive away.

'Well, talk about the gipsy's warning,' she said aloud. 'What on earth was all that about?'

She thought she understood. Genevieve was jealous! The woman shared a home with her brother. That pleasant arrangement would probably come to an end when Ambrose married. She was a little rattled by this mention of the mysterious Marie-Angele, though. By the sound of it she was a former girl friend who had taken it badly when the relationship came to an end. But if Genevieve had hoped to turn her off by mentioning his old girl friends, she had failed miserably. Of course Ambrose would have had other relationships in the past. He must be close to thirty years of age. It was only to be expected.

If Ambrose invited her out again, she would certainly go. Whether or not she would mention Genevieve's visit was another thing entirely. She would first have to wait and see how things turned out.

Meanwhile, Tom and Christina returned home, relaxed and happy after their evening out.

'Anything happen while we were gone?' Christina asked automatically, her mind on possible minor accidents or temper tantrums.

She was puzzled when she learned that Genevieve had come over.

'What on earth? Surely she isn't thinking of having us over for a meal again, so soon after the last time. Anyway, she could have phoned if that's all it was.'

'Quite the opposite!' Kat told her. 'In fact, she came to warn me off.'

Christina's jaw dropped.

'Do you mean to tell me that she doesn't want you to see any more of Ambrose? How ridiculous. He's a grown man and can make up his own mind about whom he takes out.'

'I think it was the other way round, really. She thinks I should get lost before I get my heart broken, or some such nonsense.'

'Nonsense is right!'

Christina was indignant on her younger sister's behalf.

'Anyway, what does it matter? You're going home shortly and I doubt if the pair of you will ever meet again.'

'That's what I said,' Kat said stoutly, and the subject was dropped.

The next morning, Christina took a

mysterious phone call. Kat had heard
the phone ring but of course had not
gone to answer it as her sister was in the
house. She could hear a muffled voice
coming from the kitchen so she hovered
outside the door, in case the call was
from Ambrose, wanting to speak to her.
Unable to bear the suspense she walked
into the kitchen, on the pretext of
getting a drink of water, and this
seemed to throw her sister into a tizzy.

'Look, I'm sorry. I can't talk now.'

There was a pause.

'Yes, yes, I'll get on to that right away.
Talk to you soon. 'Bye!'

She hung up the receiver and turned
to Kat with a bright smile.

'Everything all right?'

Kat knew that look of old.

'Everything is all right with me, but
how about you? You're hiding something, aren't you?'

Christina went pink, but she was
saved from answering when the phone
rang again. Kat decided to hang around
in case it was the same person on the

other end. Call her nosey, but she wanted to know what was going on.

'It's Ambrose, for you,' Christina hissed, passing the phone to her.

'Ambrose! How lovely to hear from you!'

Kat was deliberately welcoming. She was determined to show Genevieve that she refused to be dictated to.

'You sound happy this morning, cherie.'

'Do I? Well, of course, I'm on holiday, aren't I? Why shouldn't I be happy?'

'Exactly. Now perhaps I shall make you happier still. I am going to the casino tonight. Perhaps you would like to come with me.'

Kat accepted at once, and after agreeing on a time for him to collect her, she ran to find Christina, who had gone upstairs to make the beds.

'I've always wanted to visit a casino,' she said, her eyes sparkling. 'Is it far away?'

'Just a few miles from Ottawa,'

Christina told her. 'It is in Quebec which is just on the other side of the river from Ottawa. One crosses over by a bridge. The casino itself is on Leamy Lake, a few miles from there.'

'Is it very grand?'

'We don't have the money to spend on gambling, so I haven't been there myself but yes, I believe it's quite magnificent.'

The same old problem reared its head.

'What am I going to wear? Ambrose says there's a dress code.'

'Now that's something I do know about. We have friends who have been there and apparently they don't let you in if you're wearing shorts or swimwear, anything like that, but jeans and trainers are permissible, so your smart trouser suit should be all right, I should think.'

Her navy trouser suit, worn over a teal green blouse which went well with her chestnut hair, was perfectly in keeping with the crowd at the casino, not that anyone would have turned a hair if she had been scantily dressed. Everyone was too intent on having a good time.

Ambrose wanted to play roulette, not for the first time, she gathered, but she herself planned to try her luck at one of the more than fourteen hundred slot machines! She joined a queue to exchange her money then wandered about, looking for a machine which was not in use. The atmosphere was electrifying, the noise, the bright lights, the hordes of happy people. She thought she knew why Ambrose liked to come here. He probably painted scenes like this, and wanted to soak up local colour.

She had lost most of her money and was about to give up and go in search of Ambrose, when her luck changed. Coins spilled out of the machine, rattling and bouncing and, overjoyed, she scooped them up and filled her coin cup and her pockets. Not wanting to be weighed down by the money she returned to the cashier, and in exchange was given a red fifty dollar bill, which she carefully put away. It wasn't a huge amount, about twenty pounds, but she felt as elated as if she had won thousands.

It was time to go looking for Ambrose. She found him seated at one of the roulette tables, placing his chips on the wheel with great deliberation. He stood up and stretched.

'Want to go for a bite to eat?'

'Yes, please.'

She was feeling rather hungry.

'What's it to be? How about the buffet?'

They filled their plates with delicious bits and pieces and managed to find a table recently vacated by a party of four.

'So what do you think of it all, cherie?'

'Marvellous!' she told him. 'And I even won a bit of money on the slot machines.'

'Good for you. Luck is not with me

tonight. I have lost more than a thousand already, I think.'

Kat was appalled.

'No, Ambrose! Do you mean a thousand dollars?'

His wry smile did not quite reach his eyes.

'What did you think I meant, a thousand chickens?'

'But it's such a lot of money.'

'Easy come, easy go.'

She picked at her food in silence. Was he really so wealthy that the loss of a thousand dollars didn't matter, or was he one of those unfortunate people who was addicted to gambling?

When they got up from the table she half expected him to say that they would go back to the roulette tables to try to win back what he had lost, but instead he yawned and said that he was suddenly quite tired, and had she seen enough? In that case, perhaps they should be on their way.

Glancing at her watch, Kat was amazed to find that it was already almost midnight. She hoped that Tom and Christina wouldn't be anxious, although probably they would be in bed by now, having given her a key to the front door. She dozed off during the ride home, and when the car stopped she looked out of the window, expecting to find herself in front of her sister's home. Instead, they had stopped outside the Legris house. It was in darkness, except for two outside lights, one over the front door, the other suspended from an iron pole at the side of the house.

'Come, cherie, let us go inside, and I shall find you a drink.'

'No, thanks, Ambrose, it's awfully late. I've had a lovely time, but now I'm about ready to turn in.'

He was looking at her intently, his face partly in shadow.

'My thoughts exactly. Come. Genevieve is away for the night. She has gone to stay with a friend in Montreal. There is nobody here to disturb us.'

He reached over and took her into

his arms, drawing her into a passionate kiss. For once this left her cold and she struggled free.

'I'm sorry, Ambrose, really I am, but I can't do this. Please, take me home.'

He frowned.

'But will there be trouble if you do not return home tonight? Sisters can be so over protective, I know.'

Kat knew she had to choose her words with care. Before tonight she would have said that Ambrose wouldn't harm her in any way, but in this situation, how could she be sure? They were far from any populated area. She could scream her head off and nobody would hear her.

'I'm sorry if I've given you the wrong impression,' she said, although she knew quite well that she had done nothing of the sort. 'It's just that I don't believe in casual affairs.'

'I suppose you are going to tell me that you have also held yourself aloof from the faithful yokel?' he sneered.

Kat was annoyed.

'His name is George and yes, we are just friends, nothing more. Old-fashioned though it may sound, I believe there should be love and commitment first and foremost.'

Ambrose stared at her in utter amazement, as if she belonged to an alien species.

'Love, yes, but commitment is only for marriage, and perhaps not then, if both parties are so inclined. I would not have thought it, cherie, but you are a little ice maiden. Yes, that is the term for such as you. I could melt that frozen exterior, if you would allow me to do so.'

He reached for her again, and in desperation she shouted, 'And what about Marie-Angele then?'

'What about her? I suppose Genevieve has mentioned her name.'

'Yes, as a matter of fact. Who is she, Ambrose?'

He sat back, with a shake of the head.

'She is my fiancée, of course. She is

in France at the moment, learning about the making of wine, but she will return in the spring, and then we shall be married.'

'Your fiancée!'

If Kat expected him to look ashamed at having been found out, she was to be disappointed.

'Did Genevieve not tell you? We have known each other all our lives. Her family lives in Montreal, in the house next to the one where we grew up. Marie-Angele and my sister were at the convent school together. There is no grand passion between us, but she will make me a very good wife when the time comes. Our backgrounds are similar, and I think that we shall spend much of the time in Montreal, where our friends are. Yes, it will be a good marriage.'

'A good marriage, when you are betraying her already!'

He spread his hands wide.

'But what is this talk of betrayal? We have made no vows, and I do not expect that Marie-Angele is living like a nun in France.'

'Well, all I can say is, that's not the way we see things back home,' Kat snapped. 'And I feel that you've just been using me, to fill in the time until your fiancée comes home.'

Ambrose gave her a long, unfathomable look.

'And have you not been using me, Kat? You've enjoyed our time together, have you not? I have thought that we were two adults, who are free to enjoy a night together, no strings attached. But, no, the little English miss is an ice maiden, with Victorian ideas. Come, I shall take you home.'

He turned on the ignition and Kat sank back in her seat, tears of humiliation in her eyes. Tom and Genevieve had tried to warn her, but she hadn't listened. Now she was paying the price.

13

'I didn't hear you come in last night,' Christina remarked next morning when Kat came into the kitchen, yawning. 'You must have been really late. Did you have a nice time?'

'I won fifty dollars at the slot machines,' Kat told her, accepting a cup of coffee and cradling it in her cold hands.

'That's good. Did you plough it back in?'

'No way. I know when to stop. Ambrose doesn't, it seems. He managed to lose more than a thousand dollars.'

Christina gasped.

'He must have been pretty upset.'

'Well, no, he wasn't, actually. 'Easy come, easy go' were his exact words, as I recall.'

'I wish I had a spare thousand or so

to splurge on gambling. You'll miss Ambrose when you go home.'

To her consternation, Kat burst into tears.

'I've been such a fool, Tina. I really thought he was falling in love with me, and instead he was just using me! He actually wanted me to stay the night with him. Genevieve is away for a few days, apparently.'

'So what? You turned him down, I imagine. Men are like that, Kat. I'd have thought that by now you'd have enough practice in fending off unwanted attentions.'

In actual fact, Kat had not. A few clumsy good-night kisses from the boys she'd known while she was growing up were the extent of her experience. London had been a disappointment. All the eligible men seemed to have already been spoken for. George's proposal had been her first, and that had gone down like a lead balloon.

She dabbed at her eyes with a soaked tissue, and Christina handed her the box so she could take another one. Compared with the devious Ambrose, George appeared rock solid and dependable and she had treated him unkindly. She had thought herself in love with Ambrose, but the scales had fallen from her eyes in a hurry.

'It's not just that, Tina. It turns out that he's engaged to that Marie-Angele that Genevieve came to tell me about. He has no compunction about deep involvement with other women while she's away and in fact, he seems to expect that she will do the same. Well, in my view that's being unfaithful. What galls me is the fact that he was willing to draw me into a deception like that.'

Ambrose amounted to fool's gold, and because she had been so attracted to him, she had lost George. She wouldn't be surprised if he never spoke to her again and said as much to her sister.

'Well, let's face it, you knew that this was just a holiday romance, Kat, ships that pass in the night and all that. Once you get back to real life, all this will fade, as holiday romances do. Now, how about breakfast? Those babies will come roaring down here at any minute, and then we shan't get a minute to ourselves.'

Later in the day, Kat returned to the kitchen, having tidied her bedroom. Christina was chatting on the phone when Kat entered, and she broke off to say, 'Like to have a word with Mum?'

'Mum called?'

'No, I called her. Now, would you like to speak to her or not?'

'You didn't say anything about last night, did you, about me and Ambrose?' Kat hissed.

'No, of course I didn't, and here, take this phone.'

'Hello, Mum,' Kat said.

'Hello, dear. Are you having a nice time? You'll be sorry to leave, I'm sure, but I'm so looking forward to having you back.'

'Is everything all right? What did Tina want?'

'Oh, nothing much. Just wanted to chat, that's all.'

Kat was suspicious of this but she let it go. Why would Christina be making a transatlantic call in the middle of the day when the rates were at their highest?

'You haven't agreed to sell the farm, have you, Mum?'

'No, dear. I promised you I'd wait until you came home, and that's what I'm doing.'

'And is that American still interested in buying it?'

'Oh, yes, dear, and Nigel was right. He's offered us more money. He seems quite keen. Oh, I don't think there's anything more we have to say to each other, is there? I'll hear all your news when you get home next week. Have a safe trip.'

'Why did you call Mum, Tina?' she asked her sister once she'd hung up.

'Can't I call my mother once in a while without being interrogated about it?' Christina replied, with a little smile playing around her lips.

'I know what you've done, Christina Frye! You've asked Mum to let George know that it's all over between Ambrose and me, and if he acts quickly he can catch me on the rebound.'

Christina threw back her head and laughed.

'No, honestly, Kat, you're totally off-beam! It was nothing like that at all.'

And, in spite of all Kat's pleading, that was all she would say.

The last few days of Kat's holiday passed quietly. Every time the phone rang, her heart jumped, but the calls were never for her. She certainly didn't want to talk to Ambrose again, although part of her hoped that he would at least ring to apologise. She wondered if Genevieve would call to wish her a safe journey, but that didn't happen either.

The whole Frye family came to Ottawa airport to see her off. As she already knew, the flight to Toronto would take about half an hour, and then there would be a short wait for the connecting flight to London. Jack had been promised that he would stand at the window in the departure lounge to watch the planes taking off, so after a brief hug and a kiss on the cheek, Tom said goodbye and followed his eager little son on to a suitable vantage point.

She and Christina exchanged small talk until the flight was called, and then she made her way to the waiting aircraft carrying the paperback books which her sister had bought for her, to help while away the six-hour journey. She found her seat and stowed her bag in the overhead compartment and settled down to wait for the order to fasten seatbelts. She hated the moment of take-off.

The cabin attendant was just about to secure the doors when a late passenger burst in, full of apologies. As he blundered past Kat to a seat several rows behind her, she gave a gasp of surprise.

'George! What are you doing here? I thought you were back home.'

'Can't stop now,' he panted. 'Tell you later.'

There was no opportunity for Kat to talk to George during the flight. The plane was full and so they couldn't sit together even if they'd planned to. Just as well, Kat thought. Probably George wouldn't want to sit with her after their ignominious parting.

However, there were unanswered questions in her mind. As far as she knew, George had rushed back to England some days earlier, so what was he doing on the same plane now? And if their travelling together was deliberate, why hadn't he met up with her in the airport lounge? Was he afraid that she would run off, refusing even to speak to him? This was all very awkward, and it would be worse when they reached London.

As things turned out, everything fell into place quite naturally. As Kat followed the stream of disembarking passengers, George strode up behind her and took her firmly by the elbow.

'Where did you spring from?' she demanded, as he steered her towards the luggage carousel.

'I don't know what you mean. You saw me board the plane. I was sitting just a few rows behind you.'

'Yes, you do know what I mean,' she said crossly. 'When I came home that night, Christina said you'd left, so how did you manage to pop up again like this?'

'I don't think she told you I'd left Canada, Kat. When I realised that you didn't want me around, I simply went to Toronto and stayed there until it was time to come home. You should have been there with me instead of going out with that fancy artist chap. I did a lot of sightseeing and I even took a trip to Niagara Falls, which isn't far from there. It's where the honeymoon couples go,' he added meaningly.

'All that must have been expensive.'

'Oh, I didn't stay in a hotel, Kat. I stayed with Aunt Martha.'

Kat frowned.

'I didn't know you had an Aunt Martha.'

'Of course you did. She's Dad's older sister, who married a Canadian Air Force pilot and went out there as a war bride. You must remember her coming to stay with us a few years ago.'

Kat had a dim recollection of a kindly woman who had come to Stoneygates Farm when they were children, distributing sweets which seemed very exotic to them all, being quite different from anything they had seen before.

'She's over eighty now, and she doesn't like to travel abroad any more, so of course I couldn't leave Canada without seeing her. She was delighted to see me, too, unlike some people I could mention!'

'Oh, George!'

Kat began to feel very miserable indeed. Now she was back in England and about to pick up her ordinary life again, Ambrose Legris seemed as far away as a dream.

'Of course I was happy to see you, but it was so unexpected, that's all.'

'That was patently obvious,' he grunted.

Kat felt it was time to change the subject.

'Are you going straight home?'

'I certainly am. I can't wait to fall into my own bed. It may be nine o'clock in the morning here but in Canada it's four in the morning and that's what my body is telling me.'

Without putting it into words, they accepted the fact that they'd be travelling home together. Kat admitted to herself that it was good to have George by her side as they boarded the shuttle bus to the railway station and went on from there by train.

'And now I suppose we'll have to wait for ever for a bus,' Kat said wearily as they got off at their local station.

She was shivering with cold and exhaustion. Was this journey never going to end?

'Not on your life!' George told her.

'We're going to do this thing in style. I don't care if we have to mortgage the farm!'

He hailed a taxi and threw their luggage inside.

When the taxi rolled into the yard at River Farm, the kitchen door flew open and Rose rushed into the yard, her arms outstretched. Gyp was right behind her, yelping hysterically.

'Welcome home, dear, welcome home!'

George paid off the taxi and smiled at Rose.

'I couldn't bear to sit down for another minute! I'm going to walk home over the fields. You won't mind if I leave my suitcase here, will you? I'll come back tomorrow and pick it up.'

Was Kat imagining it, or did a certain meaningful glance pass between George and her mother?

But Rose simply said, 'That's right, dear, we can talk then,' as she turned to shepherd Kat into the house.

'Just look at you, Kat Ingram, white

as a sheet. I'm going to make you a nice hot cup of cocoa, and then it's off to bed with you, my girl.'

It was wonderful to be back in her own bed again. As she drifted off, she wondered why her mother wanted to talk to George. She hoped that there wasn't to be a post mortem on what had happened in Canada.

14

George found his father in the kitchen at Stoneygates, frowning over a bill which had just come in the post.

'Well, then, here you are, lad. I think you'd better have a word with that there vet. Had to call him out last week 'cos poor old Daisy had a hard time delivering her calf, but this bill says he came twice, which he never did.'

'His office manager made a mistake, I expect. That's the trouble with computers. Press the wrong key and they go haywire. Daisy all right?'

'Yes, yes. A nice little heifer. There should be tea in that pot. Sit yourself down and tell me how it went, lad.'

'Not so well, Dad. Looks like I made things worse by making the grand, romantic gesture.'

'How's that, then?'

'When I got there I found Kat had

taken up with some chap who lives near Christina's place. She seemed to be out with him morning, noon and night. So I cut my losses and went to see Aunt Martha.'

'So how is the old girl? She'd be pleased to see you, I know.'

'Sends her love. Anyway, here we are, back to square one.'

'I see it hasn't spoiled your appetite, lad,' John Logan said.

George had absentmindedly polished off a whole plate of biscuits.

'Sorry, Dad, I wasn't thinking.'

'That's young love for you. Never mind, you're home now, and this other chap will be out of the picture, I expect. Don't give up hope yet, lad.'

'The thing is, I've got some very unpleasant news to tell Kat and her mother, about River Farm. You know what they say about people shooting the messenger? I'm afraid that what I have to say will finish me with Kat once and for all.'

'Don't be too sure about that,

George! I've got a few cards up my sleeve. You're not the only one with bright ideas, you know.'

His father refused to say more, and George trudged upstairs and fell into bed. Tomorrow could take care of itself.

★　★　★

It was early morning in Canada. Christina had washed and dressed a soaking wet Lucy and strapped her into her high chair, where the child sat happily chewing on a piece of toast. Tom had come downstairs, ready to go to work as soon as he had eaten his breakfast. Christina handed him a cup of coffee with one hand and scrambled two eggs with the other.

'They'll be home by now,' Tom remarked. 'I think Kat enjoyed her stay, don't you?'

'I don't know. I wish we'd never given that beastly drinks party, then Kat wouldn't have got involved with Ambrose Legris. Then when George turned up the two of them might have fallen on each other's necks and lived happily ever after.'

'Not necessarily. You can't live other people's lives for them. You certainly shouldn't blame yourself just because you planned a party in Kat's honour.'

'No, I certainly shouldn't. But it was your idea in the first place, remember? Introduce Kat to a few of the neighbours, you said.'

'Did I? Never mind, it's water under the bridge now. What I'm more concerned about is how your mother — and Kat, of course — is going to react to what George has to say about Nigel.'

'I still can't believe that Nigel would do such a thing, Tom.'

'I can! I know he's your brother, but I've never trusted the guy.'

Christina put the frying pan in the sink and left it to soak. She would have given anything to have hopped on a plane and gone to River Farm to help sort this mess out. She still thought of it as home even though she had been a married woman living in Canada for a number of years. Instead, she had to sit here with her two small children, waiting until someone saw fit to tell her how the saga ended.

She came to with a start. Lucy was gleefully emptying the contents of a glass into her bowl of cereal. Another busy day was about to begin!

Back home in England, fate was continuing to play its hand.

'I'm coming with you, lad.'

George gazed at his father in amazement.

'It's all right, Dad. I can manage on my own, but thanks anyway.'

'I said, I'm coming with you. Your brother can manage here.'

It was strange to see John Logan dressed in Sunday clothes in the middle of a weekday morning.

Accompanied by Shep, they walked over the hill to River Farm, treading the worn path as neighbours had always done for time out of mind. The two men joined Rose and Kat at the kitchen table, ready for a council of war.

'Rose and Dad know this bit,' George began, 'but you don't, Kat, so I'll begin at the beginning, if that is all right with you, Rose?'

Rose nodded, her eyes bleak. George cleared his throat.

'Well, as you know, Kat, when your mother wanted to know if you could afford to hire another man to work here, Nigel looked over the account books and said that the farm was in a bad way. The only option was to sell.'

Kat rubbed her eyes.

'What's all this about, Mum? You haven't agreed to sell to that American chap, have you? You promised to wait and see if we could come up with anything else.'

Rose held up her hands.

'Kat, dear, do sit still and listen to what George has to say.'

George cleared his throat again. This was much heavier going than he had expected.

'Before I went to Canada, Rose told me about the problems here. I asked her if I might show the account books to a friend of mine, an old classmate from the agricultural college. Besides being a farmer, Fred is a mathematical genius, and I thought he might be able to suggest something that Nigel missed.'

'But Nigel is a qualified accountant,' Kat protested. 'I'm sure he wouldn't make a mistake!'

'No, but he doesn't know a thing about farming methods, despite having been brought up here. I thought that Fred might have suggestions, such as cutting back on the number of animals, or diversifying or something.'

'And did he?'

George hesitated.

'Look here, this is pretty difficult for me. The fact is, Fred says that there's no way things are bad enough to force you to sell River Farm. You're certainly not making money hand over fist, of course, what farmer does, nowadays, but you are managing to keep your heads above water. Fred e-mailed me in Canada, telling me this, and that's why I called Christina. I wanted her to caution Rose not to sell the place before I came back and could tell you all this in person.'

'You're not trying to say that Nigel cooked the books!' Kat snapped. 'Nigel may have his moments, but he's not a thief!'

'I'm not talking about embezzlement, or altering the figures or anything, but when you had that initial talk with Nigel, did he actually quote you chapter and verse, Rose?'

Rose thought back to the day when Kat had been made redundant from her job.

'He said a lot of things, but I didn't grasp it all,' she admitted. 'I have no head for figures, which was why I approached Nigel in the first place. He said a lot of stuff about gross and net and capital expenditures, which muddled me completely.'

'As it was meant to do,' John Logan said, grim-faced. 'He hoped to pressure you into selling, so he could get his hands on a share of the money.'

'But he could get into big trouble over something like that!' Kat protested, still not wanting to believe her brother capable of such trickery.

'It was unethical, yes,' John Logan replied, 'but hardly anything he could be punished for. If Rose found out what he was up to and reported him to the authorities he could cover himself quite nicely by saying he was just being a good son, trying to help his widowed mother by advising her to give up farming and lead an easier life. And of course you never would have reported your own son, would you, Rose?'

Rose shook her head sadly.

'And that, of course, was what he was counting on,' John concluded.

There was a long silence as Kat mentally rehearsed a few choice words that she would like to say to her brother. She got up and put her arms round her mother.

'Never mind, Mum,' She said softly. 'Now we know that you don't need to sell, we can make a go of it together. If it's all right with you I won't look for another outside job. I'll stay here and help run the farm.'

'Thank you, dear, I knew I could rely on you. The only thing is, I shan't be here much longer. I'm moving away shortly.'

'But why? Where are you going, Mum?'

John Logan stood up and went to stand beside Rose.

'She's not going very far, are you, love?'

Smiling, she lifted her eyes to his.

'Kat, Rose has done me the honour of agreeing to be my wife,' John Logan announced.

Kat was flabbergasted. George showed no sign of surprise. He must have been in on the secret already. She managed to find her voice.

'How lovely! I'm very happy for you,

Mum. When is the wedding to be?'

Rose beamed.

'As soon as we can arrange a date! And Nigel will not be invited!'

'Come on, Kat, let's take the dogs for a walk and leave the lovebirds by themselves!' George said.

The dogs heard the magic word and raced outside eagerly, followed by George and Kat.

'You don't mind, do you?'

George looked tenderly at Kat.

'About Mum and your father, you mean? No, of course not. Mum's been lonely since Dad went, and I suppose it was the same for your father.'

'I think it will be a good marriage, Kat. They've been friends for donkey's years, and they'll be wonderful company for each other.'

'So what will happen to our house, I wonder. When Mum moves over to Stoneygates it will be left empty.'

'You said that you'll be staying on.'

'That was before I knew Mum was moving out. How am I going to support myself? There aren't many jobs going in a place like this. I hate the thought of going back to the city, but that's what I'll probably have to do.'

George scratched his head.

'Actually, I might know of a job that's going, Kat, one close enough to home that would allow you to stay in the house.'

She looked at him hopefully.

'What is it, then?'

'Housekeeper to a man I know.'

'What do you mean, a sort of glorified char lady? I don't think I'd enjoy that much, going out to work with a mop and bucket. I'm an outdoors sort of person, George. If I had to do something like that I'd rather go out gardening, or working at a stable or something.'

'You might like it if you were working for the right person,' he insisted.

'Who is it then? Do I know him?'

'Yes, you do. He's a hardworking farmer with two adorable children.'

Kat racked her brains to work out

who this might be.

'Who on earth are you talking about? I don't think I know anyone like that.'

George took a deep breath.

'I'm talking about myself, Kat. I'm asking you again, will you marry me?'

Kat gasped. This was the last thing she had expected.

'But after what happened in Canada I never thought you'd ask me again.'

'Oh, well, that's over and done with. Things have changed, haven't they? When I asked you the first time, you thought it was my way of helping you to save the farm, but there's no need for that now. Rose has found out that she doesn't need to sell, and on top of that, Dad will take good care of her. So you're a free woman now.'

'This is no more romantic than the first time you proposed,' Kay laughed. 'Once again we're standing outside in a high wind, getting out heads blown off.'

'I've had it with romance, after that trip to Canada.' George grinned. 'But I suppose a girl does expect something extra when she gets a proposal!'

He sank to his knees in the mud and looked up at her with clasped hands.

'Come live with me and be my love,' he quoted, 'at River Farm, of course. Your mother says we can.'

'Take that silly look off your face, George Logan, and for goodness' sake get up, or you'll never get that mud out of your trousers!'

'I'm not getting up until you say yes.'

'Oh, all right, then, have it your own way!'

George let out a hoot of triumph which brought the dogs rushing up to see what was going on. Kat's thoughts lingered on Ambrose Legris for a brief moment, and faded. Every woman needs an Ambrose Legris in her memory bank, but real-life romance should be built on a more solid foundation. George was everything that Ambrose was not — kind, faithful, hardworking and reliable.

A sudden thought struck her.

'You told me this farmer has two

children. Have you been keeping secrets from me, George Logan?'

He laughed.

'Those children are yet to come, Kat, a boy for you and a girl for me.'

Then arm in arm they walked back to the house, looking forward to a golden future together.

THE END

We do hope that you have enjoyed reading this large print book.

Did you know that all of our titles are available for purchase?

We publish a wide range of high quality large print books including:
Romances, Mysteries, Classics
General Fiction
Non Fiction and Westerns

Special interest titles available in large print are:
The Little Oxford Dictionary
Music Book, Song Book
Hymn Book, Service Book

Also available from us courtesy of Oxford University Press:
Young Readers' Dictionary
(large print edition)
Young Readers' Thesaurus
(large print edition)

For further information or a free brochure, please contact us at:
Ulverscroft Large Print Books Ltd.,
The Green, Bradgate Road, Anstey,
Leicester, LE7 7FU, England.
Tel: (00 44) **0116 236 4325**
Fax: (00 44) **0116 234 0205**

LOVE WILL FIND A WAY

Susan Darke

Sara is an hotel receptionist until her friend Caroline, a resident, helps her into a new job — as a secretary at her son Redvers' flower-farming business in the Scillies. When Redvers eventually whispered, 'I love you, Sara', she should have been elated. But an inner voice mocked her — telling her it would be more truthful had he said, 'I love you, *Miranda*' . . . Was he merely using her as a shield against a love that had once betrayed him?

FAR LIES THE SHORE

Marian Hipwell

Calanara was an island with a secret. What caused the rift between Tansy's mother and her grandfather? And why was the hostile Mark Harmon opposed to her plans for Whitton Lodge Nurseries? Probing past events helped Tansy to find solutions to the problems of the present, only to discover that there was no place for her on the island. Yet something about Calanara called to her and the longer she stayed, the harder it became to leave . . .

LOVE'S FUGITIVE

Rachel Ford

Exploring the French Pyrenees was meant to be a complete break for Victoria, as well as inspiration for possible future work, after her recent traumatic experiences . . . It didn't work out that way — drugged and robbed, she awoke to find herself at the mercy of Gilles Laroque! As lord of the manor he wielded considerable power: Victoria found herself trapped and made to 'pay her dues'. To an independent woman, the situation was unbearable . . .